The light went out in the second-story front bed-
room, and a moment later Morgan walked out of
our house, carrying his suitcase, his briefcase, and an
umbrella. He closed the front door and came walking toward me. I straightened up my posture in a
small but pathetic attempt to present the most inviting picture possible, not really comprehending how
much I must have resembled a scrawny, wet sheepdog with glasses. Due to the darkness, he didn't
even see me until he reached the car. His face registered a small sad grin when he laid eyes on me,
stringy hair matted to my head and glasses all
fogged up. I picked up my suitcase.

"Take me with you," I said.

Awards and Honors for
MY MOTHER THE CHEERLEADER:

ALA Best of the Best Books for Young Adults

New York Public Library Books for the Teen Age

School Library Journal Best Book

VOYA (Voice of Youth Advocates) Top Shelf
Fiction for Middle School Readers

Parade Magazine Parade Picks—
Novels Teens Will Love

MY MOTHER
THE CHEERLEADER

A NOVEL BY

ROBERT SHARENOW

LAURA GERINGER BOOKS
HARPERTEEN
An Imprint of HarperCollinsPublishers

For my parents,
Arthur and Judith Sharenow

Library of Congress Cataloging-in-Publication Data
Sharenow, Robert.
My mother the Cheerleader / by Robert Sharenow.— 1st ed.
    p.   cm.
Laura Geringer Books.
Summary: Thirteen-year-old Louise uncovers secrets about her family and her
neighborhood during the violent protests over school desegregation in 1960 New
Orleans.
ISBN 978-0-06-114898-9 (pbk.)
1. School integration—Fiction. 2. Racism—Fiction. 3. Race relations—
Fiction. 4. Mothers and daughters—Fiction. 5. New Orleans (La.)—History—
20th century—Fiction.   I. Title.
PZ7.S52967 Ro 2007   2006021716
[Fic]—dc22   CIP
                                                                              AC

Typography by Neil Swaab
❖
First paperback edition, 2009

MY MOTHER
THE CHEERLEADER

My mother was a Cheerleader, but not the type of cheerleader you're probably thinking of. She didn't become a Cheerleader until she was thirty-six years old. Sometimes her cheers came out so full of foul language that the newspapers couldn't even print the words. And on the radio and television reports, they always made sure the words of the cheers were obscure, just a mad batch of ladies' voices all mixed together and blurry.

Mother's cheerleading squad formed in the winter of 1960. That November, four first-grade Negro girls were admitted to two previously all-white elementary schools in the Ninth Ward of New Orleans. Three of the girls attended McDonogh No. 19 Elementary School on St. Claude Avenue. One of the little girls entered my own humble alma mater, William Frantz Elementary School on North Galvez Street. To protest the integration, nearly all the white parents kept their children home in a simultaneous boycott of both schools. Some of the white mothers, including my own, formed a group that gathered outside my school's front entrance every day and viciously taunted those little Negro girls as they walked into the building. The newspaper reporters dubbed them "the Cheerleaders," and the media covered the protests throughout the 1960–61 school year. My mother and the other ladies took more than a passing interest in how the news media covered their activities.

The Cheerleaders drew so much attention that even Mr. John Steinbeck wrote about them in his book *Travels with Charley*. Charley was the name of Mr. Steinbeck's large poodle. In 1960 Mr. Steinbeck took his dog, Charley, on a cross-country trip in a jury-rigged camper and wrote a book about it. Their route took them through New Orleans specifically because Mr. Steinbeck wanted to witness firsthand the situation in the Ninth Ward and the Cheerleaders.

I've always admired Mr. Steinbeck's writing. I'm sure he's a fine person and he's undoubtedly a very accomplished man of letters. However, his account of the Cheerleaders just didn't sit right with me. One passage in particular struck me as being essentially inaccurate.

> *These were not mothers, not even women. They were crazy actors, playing to a crazy audience.*

My mother was not always a good mother. In fact, she was almost never a good mother. But she *was* a mother. And she was certainly not always a good woman, but she was a woman—and a human being just like Mr. Steinbeck.

I don't blame Mr. Steinbeck for writing what he did. He saw my mother and the other Cheerleaders from the outside looking in. From that point of view, I'm sure he thought he was painting a very accurate portrait. However, I saw my mother and her friends from the inside. And I've found that people always tend to look different from that angle, when you can really get in close and get a good look at all the details that hang just below the surface.

That's why I took to writing this account of my mother and specifically her encounter with Mr. Steinbeck's friend Morgan Miller. The whole episode happened over the course of just a few days. In that brief stretch of time I learned more about my mother than I had in all my previous twelve years.

CHAPTER 2

In the winter of 1960 I had just turned thirteen years old. Not many photographs of me exist from that period . . . thank the Lord. My mother tended to reserve use of the family Brownie for important occasions—like when she bought herself a new hat. It's a miracle I didn't become a fashion photographer, considering all the pictures I snapped of her accessories. Some of my best works include "Faux Alligator Handbag on Couch," "Green Leather Belt Reclining on Chaise," and her personal favorite, "Red Pumps with Black Straps in Open Box."

To be fair, I was not the most attractive kid on the block. I had plain brown hair, pale gray-blue eyes, and glasses. I was unusually tall, flat-chested, and had yet to sprout one single hair between my legs or under my arms. I barely spoke above a whisper. And my lower front teeth were each of a slightly different height, which made the bottom rung of my mouth look like a small white saw. Still, it simply had to be damaging to my ego to know that my mother cherished photographs of her shoes more than photographs of me, her only child.

Like many young girls, I hated my own name. Louise. Louise Lorraine Collins. As you may have guessed from my physical description, I was not the most popular child. Most of the boys referred to me as "the Wheeze" or just "Wheezy."

I attended William Frantz Elementary, or I did until November of 1960, when my mother pulled me out to protest the integration of one first-grade Negro girl named Ruby Bridges. I must confess that I didn't mind one bit when my education was put on indefinite hold. I had only one real friend at school, Jez Robidoux. Like me, Jez was one of the smartest kids in our grade. But I didn't see too much of her after the school boycott took hold, because her parents made her go to an alternative school in the back room of a sad little church near the industrial canal while I worked at my mother's rooming house.

The Ninth Ward never boasted the finest of anything, and the schools were no exception. Being one of the poorest wards meant we lacked many things other neighborhoods took for granted, like sidewalks or a proper sewage system. We barely had decent water to drink, never mind a decent school. Most of the streets were a series of potholes, and the air usually carried the faint odor of leftover fish bones and the sting of sulfur from the waste that traveled along the industrial canal.

I thought the teachers at Frantz were mostly time-card-punching half-wits who were just waiting to collect a state pension. On the eve of the court-ordered integration, my sixth-grade teacher,

Miss Jollet, told the class, "This may be our last class together for quite a stretch, because the state wants to see if we can train monkeys in school." My first reaction to the news that William Frantz was to be integrated was to wonder why the Negro kids wanted to go to such a crummy school.

My mother ran a rooming house on the corner of Desire and North Galvez streets. Well, to say she ran it would be fairly generous. It pretty much ran itself with the help of an old Negro lady named Charlotte Dupree and me, as soon as I was old enough to make a bed.

I'm not sure our house had an official style like Victorian, Italian, Modern, Shotgun, or the like. It was just a plain pea-green wood house with white trim featuring three stories, six bedrooms, two bathrooms, one kitchen, and one large parlor in the front that my mother called "the Music Hall" because it housed the piano. Several of the original roof shingles were missing and had been patched with mismatched replacements. The pea-green paint peeled almost everywhere, and the whole structure seemed to sag in the middle from the heat. A set of concrete steps led up to the front door, and a small sign attached to a post on the front lawn announced:

ROOMS ON DESIRE
Clean Accommodations
No Pets
Vacancy

"Rooms on Desire" had only one regular boarder—a seventy-six-year-old shut-in named Cornelius Landroux. Mr. Landroux's health had been in steep decline since his arrival four years earlier. He was missing both his legs because of diabetes. His eyes didn't see very well and he had an unpleasant disposition. I guess if I were a seventy-six-year-old legless diabetic stuck in one room, I might not be too cheerful either. His children couldn't afford a proper old folks' home, and none of them had room to keep him. So for ten dollars a week he lived in the back room of the second floor and was given three hot meals a day cooked by Charlotte or me.

Our duties also included twice-daily bedpan cleaning. Serving a meal to Mr. Landroux was never rewarding, but changing his bedpan was simply horrifying. He'd ring a small bell that he kept on his bed stand and then watch as Charlotte or I did the emptying.

Mr. Landroux bore an unquenchable hatred for the St. Louis Cardinals baseball team. Apparently, he was a prospect with the team when he was a young man, but he never made it to the big leagues. Every single day, summer or winter, he would inquire if the Cardinals had lost. If they lost, it was a good day. Given that most of the year the Cardinals didn't play—and when they did play, they won the majority of their games—Mr. Landroux almost never had a good day.

Charlotte and I dutifully endured the bedpan cleanings and Mr. Landroux's nasty disposition, because the $520 he brought in represented nearly one third of our annual income. As much as I hated him, I prayed for Mr. Landroux's good health and long life, because I had no idea how we'd get along without him.

Mother also did a fairly steady business with truck drivers who were looking for a friendly haven while passing through the city. Truck drivers were sort of her specialty. If I had been going to amend our sign, I would have added: *Truckers Welcome*. I always had to keep a stock of beer in the ice bin for the truckers. I also learned the fine art of making myself invisible on a moment's notice. But I was a born snoop, and there was rarely anything that happened inside the walls of Rooms on Desire that I didn't know about.

Mother spent the particular afternoon of Morgan Miller's arrival in much the same way she spent every other afternoon—lounging in the rocking love seat in the backyard, slowly drinking an entire decanter of her famous lime julep. December is a hot month in New Orleans. Even in the coolest weather, Mother never missed her afternoon repast. Mother's famous lime julep recipe went something like this.

> Chop three limes into half-inch pieces.
> Place limes in glass decanter.
> Add one and a half pints of bourbon.
> Fill the rest of decanter with ice.
> Add one or two mint leaves for show.
> Stir.

It was one of the very few things she prepared by herself in the kitchen. Most days she mixed the lime julep at one o'clock and then spent the rest of the afternoon rocking in the love seat, listening to the radio through the kitchen window until the decanter was empty save for the two mint leaves and a few stray pieces of lime.

I noticed she was asleep around two thirty when I came downstairs via the kitchen to read *Jane Eyre* in the Music Hall. I'd already read the book twice. Jane was my favorite literary heroine, probably because I associated my plight with hers—a poor but incredibly bright and sensitive girl who was forced to live in an old house with a crazy woman.

Something about the way the sun was hitting my mother that day, dappling through the leaves from the tree above, made her look very peaceful. I stopped for a moment and watched her chest gently rise and fall. Small sweat beads dotted her cheeks just below her eyes. Despite her harsh ways my mother was beautiful, from her curled blond hair to her full lips, which barely needed lipstick, they were so red. She was tall, with long shapely legs, and she always carried herself with an unusually feminine air, back and neck perfectly poised like a proper princess, hips swaying like a burlesque queen.

She was particularly exhausted that day because of an encounter the night before with Royce Burke, one of her regular "gentleman callers." Tall and broad, with a long chin and short black hair, Royce worked as a mechanic at a filling station and garage near the canal. Something about his face, the heavy brow and the long chin, reminded me of an etching of a prehistoric man that I saw once in a book on natural history at the library. Mother hinted that Royce belonged to a "secret society" dedicated to preserving the southern way of life. At the time I didn't know very much about the Ku Klux Klan. But based on what I did know, I wasn't surprised that Royce Burke might be a member.

Royce had a younger sister named Haley, who was confined to a wheelchair due to a childhood bout of polio. Their parents had passed on, so Haley lived with Royce and he looked after her as best he could. I guess tragedy can either soften you or harden you. In Royce's case, the misfortune of losing both of his parents and needing to tend to his crippled sister had embittered him to the rest of the world, like he needed to let everyone know just how mean life could be.

On Saturday, the night before Morgan Miller's arrival, Royce had stumbled into the house around ten thirty. I heard him banging around in the Music Hall. He spoke with a full-blown Ninth Ward accent, bending all words beginning with a smooth *th* into sharp little *ds*.

"Pauline—you dere?"

My mother stirred in the kitchen, where she had been smoking cigarettes and listening to the radio.

"Pauline?"

She shuffled into the room.

"Well, look what the cat dragged in."

"C'mere."

A loud kiss and then other moist sounds circled up to my room. I heard his heavy boots kick off and clatter across the floor and then the sound of clothes falling away. Royce grunted—a ragged snarl that grew more and more fierce.

"Royce . . . the shades," my mother gasped.

In these situations I tried to turn my ears to alarm mode after a certain point. Alarm mode was a system I had of blurring my hearing so I didn't have to endure the particulars. I always worried that Royce would really hurt my mother. His anger could rise fast. Many mornings after his visits, I saw bruises on her arms or legs, and once even a black eye.

I also needed to stay alert for my own protection. One night several weeks earlier, I had left my door open a crack. Royce stumbled upstairs to use the privy. By the time he reached the top of the stairs, it was too late for me to close my door all the way. I didn't want to risk drawing his attention. So I lay under the covers, still as I could, and waited. I heard him sway down the hall, past the toilet. The floor creaked in front of my door. I could hear him breathing and then the door slammed open.

Royce flipped on the light, all bleary-eyed. I do believe he thought he was in the privy at first. But when his eyes adjusted and he saw me, his mouth curled up in a grin. He looked down at himself. He was naked from the waist down. He let the silence hang for a moment, trying to make eye contact with me. I looked down at my pillow.

"Nothin' to be scared of here, little girl," he said.

He caught the look of horror and fear on my face and started to laugh. His laugh got harder and deeper until he couldn't control himself. He lost his balance and fell over onto the floor, landing with a hard, fleshy thump. By the time he hauled himself back up, he was too drunk and tired to bother any more with me.

I suppose most girls who grow up without knowing their father spend countless hours imagining what he must be like. They picture some elusive Prince Charming who was driven away by dire and mysterious circumstances. Not me. Because of Royce and the other men who came in and out of my mother's life, I knew beyond a shadow of a doubt that Prince Charming didn't exist.

Now, as I watched through the window as the breath made my mother's chest rise and fall in a gentle wave, all these thoughts shot through my mind. Prince Charming. My evil and unknown father. Royce Burke. Lime juleps. My mother's perfect lips, so different from my own. The glow of the sun hitting her face through the leaves.

Then I heard a car pull to a stop in front of the house. I stepped into the hall, where I could see through our front window into the street. At first the bright yellow sunlight coming in the windows blinded me. When my eyes adjusted, I could see the outline of a man stepping out of a blue 1956 Chevy Bel Air.

CHAPTER 3

Most of the men I observed in the Ninth Ward walked with just the slightest limp of defeat, as if the heat and their limited prospects had permanently hobbled them. Right away I could tell there was something different about this one. Something about the easy confidence of his stride, the way his arms dangled free, like he was unusually comfortable in his own skin and with the world in general.

He shut the front door of the Chevy with a friendly little shove, like he was patting an old friend on the back, and then he stretched his arms up over his head. Tilting his head back, he closed his eyes and let the sun fall on his face, then rolled his neck like he was trying to work out some kinks.

He wore beige chinos, a blue cotton shirt, and brown lace-up shoes, not flashy by any stretch, but not too plain either. In those first moments I probably would have put his age somewhere north of my mother's, late forties or maybe fifty. Neat furrows ran through his dark-brown hair, but it was his eyes that really gave me pause. They were sharp blue and rimmed by crow's-feet that gave him a genial expression even though he wasn't smiling.

His Chevy was practical but sporty. The chrome trim showed he possessed a sense of style. He opened the trunk and pulled out a cloth suitcase and a worn leather briefcase. As he moved toward the house, I instinctively patted down my ratty old capri pants and white button-down shirt, trying to will my hands into a hot press. He knocked on the door and stepped inside. I held back a second, watching from a distance. He looked up the staircase.

"Hello? Hello?"

I took a deep breath and stepped forward.

"Yes, sir?"

He smiled as I approached.

"You're the innkeeper?"

"Among other things."

"I'm looking for a room to rent. You have any-thing available?"

I tried to catch a whiff of his accent. He didn't sound like a Yankee. His voice carried traces of a rounded Southern lilt, but not a full-blown Louisiana drawl.

"Are you a reporter?"

He looked at me funny and replied, "Are you?"

"No."

"Well, neither am I," he said.

"Good. My mother doesn't allow reporters. Stir up too much trouble."

"Probably a smart policy, then."

I hesitated before asking the next requisite question, because it always embarrassed me to ask. But then I asked, because if I didn't and it turned out to be the case, I'd catch hell from my mother.

"Are you with the FBI?"

He laughed hard at that one and replied, "Are you?"

"No."

"Well, neither am I," he said. "But between the two of us, I'd say you'd be the more likely candidate, given your inclination toward interrogating people."

I blushed. "I don't like to ask, but my mother doesn't want any trouble and we've gotta be careful these days."

"I'm a visitor. Visiting family. My brother and his family live on St. Claude, not too far from here."

"Are you from New Orleans?"

"Originally, but I haven't been back in quite a long stretch of years."

"How many days will you be needing the room?"

"Three, maybe four."

"It's $2.50 per night, not including meals."

"That sounds fine."

"Breakfast is fifty cents extra. Dinner's available on request."

"I think I'll just start with the room before I order my entrée, if that's all right?"

I giggled.

"Do you have any bags you need help with?" I asked.

"Just these," he said, lifting his bags. "And I think I can manage."

He gestured at my book. "How do you think things will wind up for Jane at Thornfield?"

"Huh?"

"Jane Eyre," he said, nodding at the book.

"Oh, I've already read it twice. So I know what's going to happen."

"Pretty advanced stuff for a girl your age."

"My mother said I was reading headlines from *The Times-Picayune* when I was two and a half." As soon as the words escaped my mouth, I regretted saying them. I didn't want to appear to be bragging.

"Good that you moved on to literature. The news can be fairly depressing."

"The room's right up here."

I led him to the big room on the second floor at

the front of the house, overlooking Desire. It wasn't much, but it was the best room we had.

"You've got towels in the closet. And the privy's just down the hall on your left."

He walked to the window and looked out. He breathed in the air, as if he were trying to capture something in his nose that was just out of reach.

"I'm going to need the money for the first night up front."

"Oh, sure," he said, fishing his wallet from his back pocket. He counted out three dollars. "Consider the fifty cents a down payment on some eggs."

I tucked the money into my back pocket.

"Is there anything else I can help you with?"

"Well, it'd be good to know my innkeeper's name."

"Louise. Louise Collins."

"Morgan Miller," he said, extending his hand. I was just starting to enjoy the feel of his warm firm grip when I heard the first ring of the bell from upstairs. My face and heart sank. The bell rang again, more insistent. And again.

"I get the impression that bell is ringing for you."

"Duty calls," I said.

The ringing continued to sting my ears as I exited the room.

My mind raced as I climbed to the third floor. Who was Morgan Miller? He seemed completely unlike any man who had ever stayed with us. I wanted to know everything about him.

When I reached his room, Mr. Landroux angrily shook the bell like he was wringing a chicken's neck. I noticed with sharp relief that the bedpan was empty and resting on his nightstand. Then my mind froze as I realized he might've soiled the bed outright. It had happened before.

"It's about time!" he said as I entered. "I've gotta get to Louisville!"

"Louisville?"

"A scout from da Red Sox called my pa and said dey were interested. Giving me a contract with deir Triple A club for da rest of da season as long as I can pay my own way to Louisville."

Charlotte used to call Mr. Landroux "a little off

his nut," which never made a lick of sense to me, but it sounded funny whenever she said it. Is anyone ever "on their nut"? My mother called these episodes in which he retreated into his past "spells." The more he embraced the past, the more distant the present became. He frequently forgot our names and more and more often referred to Charlotte and me as Mammy and Four Eyes respectively.

"I need to get up da money for my bus fare to Kentucky."

"Mr. Landroux, it's me, Louise. You're not living with your pa anymore. You're in my mama's rooming house in New Orleans." Whenever these spells took hold, Charlotte recommended that we keep reminding him of the most basic elements of his present-day life to try and coax him out of the past. "Your son, Dennis, brought you here to live with us."

"Don't you see what kind of opportunity dis might be? Dey've got no hitters on da big club."

"Mr. Landroux, it's 1960 . . ."

He picked up the bedpan and threw it at me.

I ducked and it clattered against the back wall. He used his arms to maneuver himself out of bed.

"Please, Mr. Landroux . . ."

I tried to pin him down, but it was too late. Despite his failing health, he still had some power in his upper body when he got his anger up. He twisted himself out of bed and landed on the floor with a thud.

"Now I'm never gonna make da bus," he wailed.

"It's 1960, Mr. Landroux. Please . . ."

I attempted to lift him up, but his resistance made it impossible. Mr. Landroux's face reddened as he fought me off. Thick veins bulged from his neck under the strain. My nose pressed against his back as I tried to lift him. He smelled stale, like the inside of a musty old steamer trunk.

Suddenly I felt a gentle tap on my shoulder and turned to see Morgan Miller. He gestured for me to step aside.

"Steady there, old-timer," Morgan said.

Mr. Landroux attempted to slap him away, but Morgan grasped him firmly under both armpits and gingerly lifted him off the ground. Mr. Landroux writhed in his grasp and even landed a light slap across Morgan's face as he placed him back on the bed. Mr. Landroux continued to fight, but Morgan held him down, firmly pinning his arms and shoulders.

"Get your hands offa me!"

"Just calm down now," Morgan said.

Finally, some of the energy seemed to drain out of Mr. Landroux and he stopped flailing and just stared hard at Morgan, his eyes all wild and angry.

"Here you go," Morgan said. "Let's just simmer down, okay?"

"Simmer down? How am I ever going to show dem Cardinals what a mistake dey made if I don't get down to Louisville?"

"The St. Louis Cardinals?"

"Yes, dem goddamn St. Louis Cardinals. Is dere another one?"

"So you hate the Cardinals?" Morgan asked. "Well then, you'll be pleased to know they took a good whoopin' today."

"Really?" Mr. Landroux replied, relaxing enough

so that Morgan could release his grip.

"Thirteen to two, Chicago," Morgan answered, stepping back and straightening his shirt.

"Hot damn."

"Third loss in a row."

"I knew dey were due for a skid."

"Not only that," Morgan added, "Stan Musial contracted a parasite and may have to miss the rest of the season."

"Musial may miss da rest of da season?"

"That's right."

"Dat's the best news I've had all week."

"How about a glass of water?" Morgan offered.

"Dat would suit me fine."

I quickly poured a glass and handed it to Mr. Landroux. He took a sip, which seemed to snap him back to himself a bit.

"I think I need to rest a spell, Four Eyes," he said to me, placing the glass on his nightstand.

"If you need anything," I said, nodding, "just ring the bell."

Morgan and I exited the room, shutting the

door. Once we were in the hall, I turned to him.

"I could've handled that," I said, thrilled and embarrassed.

"I know."

"But thank you."

"Don't mention it." He winked. "I'm a Giants fan."

I laughed.

"Any chance of scaring up a glass of lemonade?"

CHAPTER 4

Rain comes fast, hard, and often in New Orleans. And rain it did as Morgan and I made our way back downstairs. There was no prelude: The wind and rain arrived together, sweeping in against the roof and windows like a bag of marbles dropping against a tile floor. We both stutter-stepped at the sound and laughed.

"I almost forgot how much the rain can take you by surprise down here," he said. "Where I live, the rain can practically come and go without anyone even noticing."

We continued down.

"Where do you live?"

"New York City. Manhattan, to be specific."

"I always wanted to go to New York." I searched for something clever to say but drew a blank. The best I could come up with was "It sure looks like something."

Ugh. I wanted everything I said to be interesting or provocative. I cursed myself for being so dull. Dull, dull, *dull*.

"It *is* something," he replied, "but sometimes I'm not sure what."

Just before we reached the kitchen, I heard her voice.

"Louise! . . . Louise!"

I entered the kitchen to find my mother drying her hair with a small dish towel. The rain had flattened her hair and soaked through her red pineapple-print dress.

"Louise, honey, could you run up and get your mother a proper towel before I flood the whole downstairs?"

She noticed Morgan standing behind me and straightened up.

"Oh, excuse me, sir. Louise, why on God's green Earth did you not tell me we had a guest? Please forgive my daughter's rudeness, Mr. . . . ?"

"Morgan Miller." He stepped forward and shook her hand.

"Charmed," she said, holding his grip for an extra moment.

"And let me assure you, your daughter has been a wonderful and very professional hostess."

A miniature sun glowed inside me.

"Yes, she is quite a child."

I hated her at that moment for calling me a child.

"I'm Pauline Collins," she continued. "Welcome."

The moisture from the rain made the dress cling to the contours of my mother's curvaceous figure. I noticed Morgan's glance quickly travel up and down her body, then just as quickly return to her face. She flashed a grin.

If I could've asked the Lord for one miracle at that very moment, it would've been to sprout woman-size breasts on the spot. Not even the most desperate adolescent boy would be caught staring at my washboard.

"Will you be staying with us?"

"Just for a few days."

"He's visiting relatives," I chimed in, desperate to prove that I knew things about him that she didn't. "He grew up here."

"How lovely—you're a native."

"I was just going to get Mr. Miller some lemonade."

"What a charming idea," she said. "Why don't you fetch us both a glass after you get my towel, while I show Mr. Miller the Music Hall."

With that she took Morgan by the arm and left me alone in the kitchen. The blood rushed up my neck and into my face. The thought of my mother and Morgan in the Music Hall made me tingle with outrage. I didn't know much about Morgan Miller at that point, but I did know that he was handsome, kind, and witty, and he lived in New York City. That was more than enough for me. All my instincts made me want to do whatever I could to keep my mother away from him.

I entered the Music Hall carrying a tray with a pitcher of lemonade, three glasses, and a towel, trying to look poised and professional. I carefully placed the tray on a side table. My mother stood by the piano, spinning one of her repertoire of dubious family legends. She almost always greeted a new guest with a story about the origins of the piano.

"This piano has been in the family since before the Civil War. According to family lore, my great-granddaddy used to play 'Dixie' for the soldiers as they marched off to join the fight. Many of those boys who came back used to seek out my great-granddaddy to tell him that the memories of his sweet melodies helped get them through the worst battles—Gettysburg, Antietam, Bull Run . . ."

I rolled my eyes, thinking, She's on her own *bull run* right now, wishing I could say it out loud.

I didn't know very much about my family history.
Most of what I knew came from Charlotte Dupree,
not my mother. According to Charlotte, my
mother's grandparents arrived in New Orleans
from Ireland at the turn of the century, a good
thirty-plus years after the war had ended. She var-
ied the story of the piano depending on the audience. Sometimes it came from her grandfather's
burlesque house. Sometimes it was a gift from a
member of the French aristocracy who gave it to
her after staying at Rooms on Desire. I believe she
gave it the Civil War spin this time around because
it had the greatest historical depth and she sensed
Morgan had an education.

"I've always been a great believer in the healing
power of music," she continued.

"I'm a music lover myself."

"Please tell me you like Peggy Lee."

"Why sure," he said. "She's a very fine vocalist."

"I just love, love, love Peggy Lee. We share a
birthday. May twenty-sixth—I won't tell you the
year. I've always felt that we were kindred spirits,

she and I. Both being blond and both being born on May twenty-sixth. Everyone will tell you: I'm a real nut when it comes to music. Radio's almost always on in here."

"I'm a big fan of the Weavers. Ever listen to them?"

"'Goodnight Irene'! That one's a beauty. I'm not sure how partial I am to the rest of their stuff. It's a little too folky for me. I mean, I don't know why anyone would want to sing about having a hammer and hammering in the morning and in the evening and all that. Never made much sense to me at all. I mean, who in their right mind likes to hammer all day?"

Morgan chuckled, charmed. I handed my mother a towel.

"Why, thank you, dear," she said, "but I'm almost completely dry."

She dabbed her forehead once and handed it back.

I poured three glasses of lemonade.

"I hope you'll be joining us for dinner, Mr.

Miller. I'm known far and wide for my paneed chicken and creamy garlic greens."

Of course, she meant to say that she was known far and wide for Charlotte's paneed chicken and creamy garlic greens.

"Well, I'm planning to drop in on my brother and his family this afternoon," he said. "But they don't know I'm coming, so maybe it'd be a good idea to have dinner plans."

"Wonderful," my mother said. Then she noticed me taking a seat on the edge of the couch.

"Aren't you meeting your little friend Jez Robidoux this afternoon?" she asked.

"No," I replied flatly.

"Well then, it's probably a good time for you to check the larder to see what ingredients we need to pick up for tonight."

Reluctantly, I slunk off to the kitchen. Once inside, I pressed my ear hard up against the door.

"When was the last time you visited New Orleans?" she asked him.

"It's been more than twenty years."

"Twenty years! Why, you must hardly recognize the place."

"Hasn't changed much, from what I can tell so far."

"Well, if you'd like me to show you around . . ."

"I might take you up on that," he said. "But right now I think I'm gonna try to catch up with my brother."

"Of course. I usually serve dinner around seven."

"That suits me fine."

I heard them rise and move to the door.

I reacted quickly, bolting out the back door and grabbing my bike out of the shed. I had a light-blue 1955 Schwinn Spitfire that I used for surveillance missions. As I mentioned before, I was a first-class snoop, and Morgan Miller was worthy of my highest level of observation.

A small path ran from the shed along the side of the house to the street. I ran with my bike to the edge of the front of the house and peered around the corner just in time to see Morgan get back behind the wheel of the Bel Air. I waited for him to pull out before emerging from my hiding spot. The car drove toward St. Claude. I heard my mother calling for me from inside as I pedaled with all my might in hot pursuit.

CHAPTER 5

After a few weeks of the school boycott, most of the white parents in our ward started sending their kids to alternative schools. My mother seized the opportunity to have me working full-time around the house. Her political stand on segregation allowed her to pawn off nearly all her housework on me. By the third month of the boycott I was pretty much doing anything and everything having to do with tidying and cleaning the house and tending to the guests.

Besides housework, I didn't have much to do with myself other than snoop. As a result, my snooping skills became finely honed during the first few months of the boycott. J. Edgar Hoover and his G-men loomed large in my imagination, rooting out Communists and other evildoers. I fantasized about becoming the first girl agent in the FBI. I even fashioned myself a pretend identification card and badge out of an old toy sheriff's star.

I learned how to eavesdrop from every nook and cranny in our house, locating through trial and error a set of key surveillance points. For instance, by lying on the floor of the third-floor closet, I could hear everything that went on in the second-floor bedroom at the front of the house. From the roof of the shed in our backyard I could peer right into the third-floor bedroom in the back. Sometimes I even used binoculars. Best of all, in the bathroom on the second floor there was a removable ventilation grate that allowed me to listen and look down into the Music Hall below without being observed.

One of my favorite activities was something I

called "search and record" missions. While cleaning a guest's room, I would meticulously take out and examine every item they had brought, marking down articles of note in a series of pocket-size spiral notebooks that I called my Spy Logs. I always kept at least one in my back pocket with a sawed-off pencil. You learn a lot about people by looking at what they pack for a trip. But I had to be extremely careful not to get caught and to return every item exactly as I had found it. I also became an expert at trailing people. If a guest interested me, I might follow them for hours, dutifully recording their movements in my Spy Log.

After pulling away from our house, Morgan's Bel Air made a right on St. Claude and headed toward downtown. I raced after him on my bike. St. Claude was the main commercial drag of our area. Sad little stores dotted the blocks, providing basic services to the community—Laundromats, pharmacies, po'boy shacks, and of course bars and liquor stores.

I believed that tracking Morgan's car would be

slightly easier than others I had tried to follow because it was perhaps the only car in our ward sporting New York license plates. Yet I quickly fell far behind in my pursuit. I furiously pumped my legs, sweat pouring out of me, but I kept losing ground. I was certain I'd lose him, when he suddenly slowed and pulled to a stop. While he parked, I slid my bike to a stop behind a parked car a block away.

Morgan stopped the engine, but he didn't move to get out of the car. I left my bike and edged up to get a closer look, crouching behind the bumper of a beat-up Ford truck parked just a few spaces behind him. Morgan stared across the street at a small grocery store. A weathered sign above the door read FRIENDLY MARKET. EST. 1915. The building featured a second story that I assumed was used as an apartment. Morgan lit a cigarette and took long, pensive drags as he watched the store. I edged forward so I could see through the front window. Inside, a tall, thin, balding man stood at the cash register, ringing up a customer. Bananas.

A box of soap flakes. Toilet paper. Canned tuna. A five-pound bag of rice.

The man at the cash register wore a thigh-length white topcoat over a shirt and tie. Morgan watched from his car for nearly an hour. In that time the bald man rang up ten customers, swept the aisles once, and in between read the sports section of *The Times-Picayune*. I noted every movement in my Spy Log.

4:05 PM—Bald man reads paper.

4:16 PM—MM lights another cigarette.

4:31 PM—Fat lady buys several packages of dried prunes.

4:46 PM—Bald man blows nose into handkerchief.

Morgan never budged. After about forty-five minutes and six cigarettes, he started the engine and drove off toward the French Quarter. I didn't follow. I knew I'd never catch him, so I gave myself a new surveillance assignment: Infiltrate Friendly

Market and observe the bald man from close range.

I retrieved my bike and leaned it against a telephone pole; then I crossed the street and boldly entered the store. It's strange to be in close proximity to someone you've been spying on from afar. It's almost like seeing a movie star in the flesh. The bald man barely looked up as I walked through the door, triggering a small tinkling bell. The newspaper he read partially hid his face.

"Need help finding anything?" he asked from behind the front page.

"Penny candy," I replied.

"Top of the first aisle," he said, gesturing with his head but still not really looking at me.

Typical groceries packed the three tight aisles that ran the length of the store, organized into broad categories: baking supplies, jarred and canned vegetables, boxed cereals and oatmeal silos. A large refrigeration unit toward the back held bottles of fresh milk, Dr Pepper, Tahitian Treat, and orange juice. There was no meat counter or fancy dairy section, just the basics. I stopped in front of the penny candy shelf, which boasted a decent selection: Pixy Stix, candy buttons, Slo Poke suckers, jawbreakers, licorice pipes, chocolate cigarettes, wax lips. Good surveillance work often involves spending money to create a viable cover. So I chose two pairs of wax lips, one with a mustache, one without, and three fireballs, and made my way back up to the counter.

I placed the items on the counter to get the bald man's attention. He lowered the paper to reveal Morgan's sharp blue eyes.

"That it?" he asked.

"Yeah," I said, handing over my five cents.

"Well, I won't be retiring on this sale," he said with a small grin, revealing that he also had Morgan's pattern of crow's-feet stamped into the corners of his eyes. I studied his face and noticed that, unlike Morgan's, the bridge of his nose and his forehead also bore deep lines, giving him a slightly strained and tired expression.

He popped my collection into a small paper bag and I exited the store. I placed the wax lips with the mustache between my teeth and held it for a moment, admiring my ridiculous visage in the side mirrors of cars as I walked back to my bike. Slowly I chewed, letting the strange sweetness run down my throat as the wax became a huge amorphous wad at the back of my mouth.

CHAPTER 6

When I got home, I found Charlotte Dupree ironing my mother's Southern belle dress in the kitchen. Made from soft brushed turquoise-colored cotton with sassy white polka dots, the dress was an exact replica of a real gown from the antebellum period. It even came with a matching polka-dot parasol. Charlotte hated ironing in general. And ironing the Southern belle dress drove her to distraction.

"She thinks she's Scarlett O'Hara on a plantation or something," she grumbled. "Blasted bodice is impossible to get flat. I don't want to be the one to tell her, but this place sure ain't no plantation and she ain't no Scarlett."

My mother loved playing dress-up, and the blue polka-dot Southern belle dress was her most prized possession. She wore the costume at fund-raising trips aimed at financing a segregated school for the Ninth Ward. The segregated South took great interest in seeing the Ninth Ward stay segregated. So, dressed as Southern belles, my mother and some of the other Cheerleaders would make trips to towns all around Louisiana and Mississippi. Once there, they'd roam the main streets collecting donations in white wicker handbaskets. Whenever a man plunked some coins in a basket, they would stay in character and demurely curtsy, bat their eyelashes, and purr, "Why, thank you, kind sir."

My mother never took me along on her fund-raising trips. That was her time to be alone with the girls. Unfortunately, I did have my own matching Southern belle dress, which she would force me into for local parades and other neighborhood events. I loathed dressing up in general, and my Southern belle dress was particularly uncomfortable to wear. When I complained, my mother would respond with genuine astonishment.

"Most girls like dressing up in beautiful gowns. I would've been thrilled if my mother had included me in something that was so much fun."

"Well, you and me aren't the same," I'd retort.

"You're right about that," she said.

"I hate it."

"This isn't about what you like or hate," she said. "Having a little belle is the ultimate accessory. It's cute. And everyone thinks so."

"I don't. So not everyone thinks so."

"Fine. Everyone but you."

We always had to wear our dresses to the Citizens' Council events. The Citizens' Council of Greater New Orleans was a civic group dedicated to opposing school integration in the city. Looking back, people tend to think that there were two sides of the line on the segregation issue in the Ninth Ward, but there weren't, at least not where I lived. Not at the beginning, anyway. Just about everyone in the Ninth Ward believed in segregation, including the Negroes. It was one of those things that you just assumed everyone agreed on or you didn't think much about. I was in the latter category. I never thought to think any other way.

Every so often the Citizens' Council had big meetings with lots of pageantry and featured guest speakers. A few days before Morgan's arrival there was a big council function at the Municipal Auditorium. Nearly eight hundred people packed the hall. A brass band played on a riser beside the stage.

After the singing of the national anthem and the recitation of the Pledge of Allegiance, the head of the council, Mr. Amos Bovell, called forward a group of mothers and daughters from William Frantz and McDonogh No. 19 elementary schools. My mother and I were part of the group that paraded down the aisle in our plantation dresses, carrying our parasols and placards that read DESEGREGATION IS A SIN and PRESERVE THE SOUTHERN WAY OF LIFE. I hated being on display with every fiber of my being. My mother basked in the attention like she was strutting down the red carpet at the Academy Awards.

Once we reached the stage, one of the ladies presented Mr. Bovell with a check for $1,647.17, the proceeds of their most recent fund-raising trip, payable to the Ninth Ward Educational Association. Mr. Bovell raised the check high over his head as the crowd cheered, and we exited the stage to the tune of "Dixie" and took our seats toward the back.

It was time for the guest speakers. The air in the hall heated up and got stale, causing me to try to fight off an escalating series of uncontrollable yawns. All I wanted to do was change out of my costume. The bodice made me itch like a crazed hound. I nudged my mother and begged her to let me go home.

"It's poor form to leave before the speakers," she hissed.

"You never really listen anyway, so why do we have to—?"

"Hush!" she cut me off, giving my hand a small sharp swat.

First to speak was a judge from Jackson, Mississippi, named Barton Floyd. A stout bald man with a thick layer of flabby skin hanging over his shirt collar, he waved his hands and pointed for emphasis with his stubby little index finger. Judge Floyd spoke at length about the "Black Monday" Supreme Court decision of May 17, 1954, that declared segregation of the races in public schools was unconstitutional.

"That ill-conceived decision triggered a racial revolution," he explained, "spearheaded by the N.A.A.C.P. and abetted by Communist subversives."

The crowd grumbled in distress. One man shouted, "We won't let it happen!" Judge Floyd wiped his brow with a folded handkerchief and then held up a newspaper.

"This is a copy of the *Daily Worker*, a Communist newspaper printed by Jewish publishers in New York City. It says, and I quote, 'The Communist Party considers it as its duty to unite all workers, regardless of color, against its common enemy—Capitalism. Racial desegregation is an essential building block to achieving our goal of a Communist society.' Unquote. Now, are we going to let the *Daily Worker* tell us how to live?"

"No!" shouted several audience members.

"Heaven forbid," another chimed in.

Judge Floyd quieted the crowd with his hands.

"It's important to remember that the Negro is not your enemy," the judge continued. "The Communists. The Jews. And other Northern manipulators. They are the ones stirring up this trouble and financing the N.A.A.C.P. The Supreme Court of this great land cannot rewrite our precious Constitution and revoke our most precious freedoms. I applaud and support your efforts here in New Orleans. You must do whatever it takes to maintain the separation of the races. Hold the line, people. Hold the line. We will win this fight, because we *must* win this fight."

The band struck up "Dixie" again, the crowd

vigorously applauded, and with that the meeting was adjourned. My mother stuck around to gossip outside the hall. With the show over, I was free to go home and liberate myself from the confines of my itchy dress.

CHAPTER 7

After Charlotte finished the laundry, we set off to buy groceries for that night's dinner. First we stopped at a poultry store in the Negro section called Antoine's Pick-a-Chick. There was a white butcher right around the corner from Rooms on Desire, but Charlotte refused to patronize that establishment. "Oh, I tried giving them my business," she explained. "and they were more than happy to take my money. But somehow whenever I'd go in there, I'd always wind up with maggots in my meat or a chicken that had been lying around for days and turned sour." There was no risk of getting spoiled meat at Antoine's. The store was just a one-room shack with a counter, a cash box, and not much else. Antoine himself took up a good amount of space inside the room. He stood about six foot six and must have weighed close to three hundred pounds. He had chalky, coal-colored skin and wore a big droopy mustache that never failed to bend up into a smile when Charlotte walked in. Inside the shack, behind the counter, dozens of live chickens roamed freely. A makeshift coop lined the side wall of the back of the building. The back door of the shack always stood open, and the chickens walked out at will into the yard, where Antoine would scatter feed throughout the day. "I like to keep dem chickens fat and happy," he explained.

Antoine allowed his customers to come behind the counter and select their own chickens. When we arrived, he grandly gestured with a wave of his arm—"Right dis way, my ladies"—and bowed to Charlotte as we passed behind the counter. Charlotte took her time observing the chickens before making her choice. "You don't want one that's moving too fast or it'll likely be too gamey," she instructed. "And you don't want one that's moving too slow or it'll likely be too fatty." She pointed out a large chicken with white feathers that to her eye seemed to be traveling at a moderate speed.

Antoine nodded. "A fine choice, as always, Miss Charlotte." Then he scooped up the chicken, put it under his arm, and carried it behind a crude wooden wall in the backyard that hid where he kept the chopping block. We met him back in front of the counter, where he returned with the headless but unplucked chicken in a paper bag. "Antoine's finest for Antoine's finest," he said, handing over the bag and taking Charlotte's money. He gave her a wink that she pretended to ignore, and we left.

Next, we stopped to buy crabs from Antoine's son, Jermaine, who sold them by the side of the road just beyond the chicken shack. Jermaine couldn't have been much older than me. He wore faded overalls and no shoes, but his hair was always neatly styled with a sharp part line dividing his tight curls. He barely said a word to us beyond "yes," "no," and "thank you kindly," and he never looked me in the eye. He sat on a small wooden stool beside an old metal washtub filled with live crabs in water that he kept shaded by an old umbrella. He caught the crabs himself in the early morning using a long piece of string with an old chicken neck tied to the end. One of the few times I heard him speak more than single words, he boasted that he had pulled up six crabs on one dip, more than any other kid in the city. "And I can still get dem to come up when near all the meat has been picked off da neck." Unlike me, he seemed to be proud of his labors, which I could never quite understand. You would never catch me bragging about how many floors I could clean or beds I could make in an hour.

Charlotte carefully selected eight crabs, making sure they were still alive by poking them with her index finger. "You never want to buy a dead crab,"

she said. "Dead meat's not sweet." The crabs
responded by flexing their claws over their heads. It
always looked to me like they were stretching after
waking up in the morning. Jermaine waited while
she conducted her inspection. One of his feet tapped
impatiently. I shot him a knowing smile, attempting
to forge an alliance. I think he knew I was trying to
catch his eye, but he quickly turned his glance to his
tapping feet and kept them there until Charlotte
was finished.

After we arrived back home, we set to work
preparing the meal. First she boiled the crabs and
cleaned all the meat out of the shells, chopping
it into a pile for crab salad. To this she added just
a pinch of salt and the juice from a whole lemon.
While she did this, I mixed together her rémoulade sauce to use for dipping—mayonnaise, sour
cream, cayenne pepper, salt, and crushed mustard
seeds.

Next, Charlotte plucked the chicken and carefully separated the meat from the bones with a sharp
little knife. She expertly cut away the flesh so as not

to leave even the smallest piece of meat behind. She reserved the bones for soup and gave the meat to me for pounding under long sheets of waxed paper.

"So who are we cooking for this time?" she asked. "Another trucker?"

"He's not a trucker," I replied a little too sharply. Charlotte raised an eyebrow.

"Oh? Then what is he?"

"I don't know," I said. "But he's not a trucker."

For emphasis I started pounding the chicken with the large wooden mallet. *Thump, thump, thump.*

"You don't have to beat the life out of it," she warned.

Charlotte's paneed chicken recipe was a closely guarded secret. She coated the chicken with bread crumbs and a mix of spices and green herbs: thyme, basil, and oregano. She also added a healthy dose of grated dry cheese and an egg "to make it all mingle and stick to the skin."

But her most unusual technique involved wrapping the chicken in raw bacon strips. She let them sit for about an hour. "Two meats that don't know each other need a chance to get acquainted," she explained, "before they're thrown in the pan together." Then she'd cook the bacon strips until they were nice and crispy. Using the edge of a cleaver, she'd pulverize the bacon and mix it into the butter in the pan before adding the chicken. "That way, the butter and the bacon stick together and gang up on the chicken," she said. One of my favorite smells in the world was Charlotte's chicken sizzling in bacon butter. I'd inhale deeply until the smell got dull in my nose. Then I'd step outside and breathe some of the outside air just so I could step back inside and let the smell hit my nose again.

Charlotte had been working for my mother since before I was born. I never knew her exact age, and she refused to divulge it. She did once reveal that she remembered the turn of the twentieth century. "I was just a little thing," she explained. "And my mother woke me up at midnight and took me down by the water in my nightgown to see the fireworks. I had never been allowed out of the house in my nightgown before." So she had to be north of sixty. Her hair was grayed around the temples and crown, but her skin was remarkably unlined and had an unusually reddish tint. She had huge cat-shaped eyes that were the deepest black and shone like glass marbles. She always dressed in neat blue, green, or gray dresses, alternating among the three.

Charlotte described herself as "a churchgoing, no-nonsense woman." She quipped, "I have to be, around here, because your mother is an *all*-nonsense woman." It was true that my mother and Charlotte had vastly different temperaments. My mother was loud. Charlotte was quiet. My mother dressed flashily. Charlotte dressed demurely. My mother rarely attended church. Charlotte practically lived at hers and even taught Sunday school there.

Unlike my mother, Charlotte was a reader. She kept two books on hand at all times, the King James Bible and a Webster's unabridged dictionary. "Between these two books," she said, "you could

explain just about everything in this wide world."
It was Charlotte who really taught me how to read
and encouraged me to keep expanding my vocabu-
lary. "The more words you know," she explained,
"the less someone will be able to trick you into
something." She conditioned me to stop reading
when I came across a word I didn't know and look
up the definition. "You keep on doing that, by the
time you get to be grown up there won't be any
words that take you by surprise and you'll be
nobody's fool."

One of the only traits my mother and Charlotte
shared was an aversion to any kind of New Orleans
slang. Neither of them replaced the words *the*, *them*,
and *there* with *da*, *dem*, and *dere*. And they both
avoided using the standard Ninth Ward greeting:
"Where y'at?"

My mother tried her best to sound like a refined
Southern lady from a Hollywood movie set on a
plantation. While my mother spoke "Hollywood
English," Charlotte claimed to speak "Bible English." I once heard her admonish her friend Julie,

who sometimes came over in the afternoons to discuss Scripture. "Jesus gave a Sermon on *the* Mount," she said, "not a Sermon on *da* Mount." Julie replied, "I don't know why y'all are making such a fuss, Charlotte. Jesus and dem didn't speak English back den anyway."

Charlotte and my mother did have another thing in common: They both closely guarded the details of their pasts. Most of the information I had gathered about each of them over the years had come from the other. My mother said that Charlotte's daddy had been a preacher at a Negro church and that Charlotte had been a rebellious child. She got into all sorts of trouble with men when she was still a teenager and had run away from home. A few years later she came back. The world outside her neighborhood had taught her some hard lessons, so she moved back into her daddy's house. She still lives there to this day. Her daddy passed on, but her mother is still up and around and is said to be nearing one hundred years old.

"Do you think I'm pretty?" I blurted out, after silently pounding the chicken for a couple of minutes.

Charlotte paused in chopping the greens and looked me up and down and nodded.

"You've got all the right parts," she said. "You'll be a pretty woman."

"You say it like it's something that's gonna happen in the future," I pleaded. "I'm asking if I'm pretty now."

"Why are you so hot and bothered to know?"

"I just am."

"You want the truth?" she asked, putting down the cleaver.

Suddenly afraid, I paused a second before responding, "Yes."

"You're cute," she said, and resumed chopping.

"Cute?" I whined. That was the wrong answer.

"You're still a little girl," she said. "You should be happy with cute. Pretty will come later. And don't be in a rush for it, either. The more you try to rush something like that, the more you risk turning into something that doesn't know what it is. Nothing looks worse than that."

"Thanks a lot." I pouted.

"If you don't want honest answers, don't ask me."

"I won't."

We prepared the rest of the meal in silence.

CHAPTER 8

My mother spent the afternoon at the Paris Beauty Shoppe on St. Claude, having her hair done and her nails painted fiery red. After setting the dining room table for three, I brought Mr. Landroux his dinner tray and then retreated to my room to get dressed. I wore my best Sunday clothes, a light-green cotton dress with a white sash and a matching white ribbon in my hair. Using a dime-store hand mirror, I applied the slightest layer of lipstick. My mother didn't want me wearing any makeup, but I had swiped a lipstick from her a year ago that I occasionally used as a one-stop makeup kit. I lightly layered my lips, just enough to give me a splash of color but not enough to look like I was actually wearing lipstick. Next, I rubbed a small amount into my cheeks as substitute rouge.

My mother returned around five o'clock and spent the rest of the afternoon picking out her wardrobe for the night. She settled on a tight red cocktail dress, aware that she could wear a red potato sack and make it look sexy. But this dress was no potato sack.

Morgan came down to the dining room at exactly the appointed time.

"You look lovely tonight," he said to my mother as he came to the table, his eyes taking in all the hot spots.

"Why, thank you." My mother blushed.

"You too, Miss Louise," he said. "I should've brought fancier duds."

"You're perfect, Mr. Miller," my mother said. "Just perfect."

He wore exactly the same clothes he had worn during the day, with the addition of a blue linen blazer. He had shaved and smelled faintly of an aftershave or cologne that was sweet yet masculine.

Charlotte's dinner of crab salad with rémoulade sauce and paneed chicken and creamy garlic greens was a smashing success. Morgan ate seconds and lavished compliments on my mother for culinary skills she did not possess. As Charlotte passed through the dining room clearing plates, she subtly rolled her eyes at me when she overheard Morgan praise the smoky flavor of the sauce. I stifled a giggle.

We finished the meal with a plate of Charlotte's homemade pralines. Before mixing in the pecans, she would sauté them with butter, just a dash of cinnamon, and crushed nutmeg, "to give them a bit of mystery." I usually ate at least six pralines in one sitting, but held myself to two that night, not wanting Morgan to think I was a glutton.

Most evenings I took my dinner in the kitchen.

Sometimes I ate with Charlotte. More often than
not I ate alone, because Charlotte liked to be home
to feed her mother. My mother never really ate any
proper meals. She'd pick at things throughout the
day without ever sitting down to a whole plateful
of anything. She never ate dinner with me unless a
guest had requested dinner. Then she would put
on a show and have us all eat in the dining room,
and act as if we did so every night. Most of those
meals were dull affairs, where I'd sit quietly and
listen to the guests and my mother talk. If she was
entertaining one of her truckers, he would typically do most of the talking, droning on about the
road, just thankful to have a set of human ears listening. But Morgan was different. He seemed to
listen just as much as he talked. And it wasn't the
kind of listening where he would just be waiting
for my mother to finish so he could start talking.
He actually seemed to be interested in what my
mother was saying; and she and I were certainly
interested in him.

"What business are you in, Mr. Miller?" my

mother inquired as Charlotte cleared the dessert plates.

"Publishing. I'm an editor."

"How fascinating. Do you do romances? Westerns? Mysteries? Do you work with anyone I might've read?" she asked.

I snickered to myself at the thought of my mother actually reading something other than her horoscope.

"Probably not. I edit mostly textbooks and technical journals. Pretty dry stuff."

"Surely you must have gotten to meet some famous writers."

"Well, I guess a few."

"Oh, I knew it. Who? Please tell! Things are so dull down here. We never get to meet anybody famous."

"Well, my work really isn't that glamorous. But I am friendly with John Steinbeck and his wife."

My head nearly exploded. Did he really mean *the* John Steinbeck?

"Steinbeck! I love Steinbeck," my mother

squealed with delight. "He's my very favorite author."

"Really?"

"Why, yes! His books make the most wonderful movies. I must've seen *East of Eden* ten times. Please tell me you've met James Dean."

"I'm afraid not," Morgan replied with a light chuckle.

"What a gorgeous man he was. He was just made for the role of Cal Trask. I cried when I heard about the car crash that took him, I really did. What about Henry Fonda?"

"Henry Fonda?"

"Did you ever meet him? He was in *The Grapes of Wrath*. That was Steinbeck too, right?"

"No, I never met him, but I did see the picture. It was quite good."

"What a wonderful actor. Those eyes of his just melt me. . . ."

"I've read *Of Mice and Men*, *The Red Pony*, *The Pearl*, and *Cannery Row*," I interrupted.

My mother's eyes bulged in surprise.

"Pretty advanced stuff," he said.

"She's quite a bookworm," my mother commented, making sure to place just the right emphasis on the word *worm* to telegraph to me just how mad she was at being upstaged and interrupted.

"What'd you think?" he asked.

"What did I think?"

"Yes. About the books?"

"I love his books," I said.

"Why?"

"Why?" I paused. "It's the characters. They're like real people. A lot of books you read have all these characters that you'd never really come across, like they're too smart or too funny or too brave. But John Steinbeck's stories are about real people, people you think you might've seen in your own life. They talk like real people talk, not like in lots of books, where they talk like some writer's idea of how people oughta talk, and . . ."

I trailed off, suddenly embarrassed. I'd never talked so much at the dinner table before. "Sorry," I mumbled.

"No. Go on," Morgan prompted me.

My mother glared at me with heat-lamp eyes.

"Well, it's as if his characters really exist some-where," I said. "Like the bums on Cannery Row, or the farmhand Lennie from *Of Mice and Men*. I feel like I know people just like that right here in New Orleans. And I guess reading those books made me think I understand those people a little better. At least I think I do."

"I think John would be very impressed by your analysis, Miss Louise." He turned to my mother. "She really is very advanced for her age."

"Yes, she's something all right," my mother replied. "She took to books like a fish to water. Ever since she was the littlest girl, book learning was just like breathing with this one. She'd read through all the kiddie books at the library by the time she was nine and then started in on the adult section. It's really quite amazing considering how long it took me to potty train her. Do you realize she was still wetting the bed at age five?"

My throat constricted so fast I nearly choked,

like I'd been bit by a water moccasin. My eyes filled
with tears. It took all my powers of self-control to
stop myself from bursting into sobs. Even if I could
have found my voice, I couldn't have rebutted what
she said, because it was true. I'd never been to a
sleepover for fear I'd have a relapse.

"Five!" Morgan gasped. "That's nothing. I wet
the bed until I was nearly eight." He winked at me.
"It's always a pleasure to dine with another former
member of the rubber sheet club."

At that moment I was absolutely convinced he
was an angel. My throat instantly relaxed and I felt
my spirit lift toward heaven. Two fantasy scenarios
formed in my mind. Either I would marry this man
or he would adopt me as his own child. Either way,
he would take me back to New York City with him
so we could discuss books all day long.

"Morgan, would you care to join me for a sherry
in the Music Hall?" my mother asked.

"That sounds nice," he said.

"Louise, I think it's time for you to help
Charlotte in the kitchen, and then it's time for bed."

Banished. I knew it was coming. She had me. I couldn't disobey her without seeming like a brat. Reluctantly, I rose.

"Will you be joining us for breakfast, Mr. Miller?" I asked.

"Not tomorrow," he replied. "I'm meeting a friend early in the morning. Maybe Tuesday."

"Say good night, Louise," my mother instructed.

"Good night, Mother. Good night, Mr. Miller."

"Good night, Miss Louise," he said.

He gallantly rose and dramatically kissed my hand. My face flushed so fast, I had to turn away and quickly retreat before he saw me transform into a beet before his eyes.

I found Charlotte drying the dinner plates as I entered the kitchen. I tried to busy myself putting away the pots and pans that Charlotte had already washed and dried, so she wouldn't notice my agitated condition. I worked fast, because I wanted to retreat upstairs so I could eavesdrop from my secret spot in the second-floor bathroom. In my haste I dropped a glass, which shattered across the floor.

"What's wrong with you?" she said.

"Nothing."

"You sure you don't have a fever or something?"

"No," I said. But I was lying.

I fetched the broom, and Charlotte swept up the broken shards while I held the dustpan. Thoughts of Morgan had somehow gotten under my skin and inside my veins, throbbing in my chest and in my head. My entire body felt hot.

"You're so red it looks like you got sunburned."

"It's nothing."

Charlotte put her hands on my shoulders.

"Then let's talk about nothing," she said.

She tried to stroke my cheek, but I abruptly turned away and dumped the broken glass into the trash can.

Charlotte put away the broom and washed and dried her hands. She kissed me on the head, put on her coat, and tied on a kerchief over her hair. I placed the last plates back on the pantry shelf.

"Louise?" she called to me.

Slowly I turned to face her.

"You look pretty tonight," she said, and then she walked out, closing the back door behind her.

CHAPTER 9

I had discovered my top-secret observation post in the second-floor bathrooms completely by accident two years earlier. As a little girl I had adopted the unusual habit of polishing my coins. Whenever I'd get any money, the first thing I'd do was take the coins into the bathroom and scrub them down with soap and hot water. For some reason I had it in my head that adding shine would increase their value. During one of my cleaning sessions I dropped a quarter down the heating grate behind the toilet. When I got down on my belly and pried open the grate, I realized that you could hear everything that went on in the Music Hall, clear as a bell. Not only that, but if I stuck my head down inside, I could actually see a little bit into the Music Hall from the ceiling grate. When I did this, the blood would always rush to my head, so I usually had to content myself with just crouching near the opening and listening.

I used my secret observation post in the second-floor bathroom very sparingly, for only the most intriguing guests. There was always a chance that a guest would need to use the toilet, and then I'd have to scramble to put the grate back in place in time. I didn't risk exposure for the likes of Royce Burke. And if anyone's clothes started to come off, I'd retreat before things got too grisly.

After Charlotte left, I quietly snuck off to the upstairs bathroom, carefully removed the grate, and listened. They were settled in the Music Hall over glasses of sherry. When I stuck my head down into the hole, I could just make out my mother sitting on the couch and a piece of the back of Morgan's head as he sat on the love seat next to her. I tried to keep my head down to watch, but had to pull myself back every few minutes when the top of my head throbbed. My mother regaled Morgan with her silly little Southern belle yarns. Some of the stories were true, most were not. But somewhere along the line the conversation took an unusual turn.

"So—is there a Mrs. Miller?" my mother asked.

"There was," he said. "We're no longer together."

"I'm sorry," she lied. "I don't mean to pry."

"No. It's all right. It's still strange for me to say it. We were married for so many years. Twenty-five, to be exact. It's funny, I never thought I'd be the type to get divorced. But I suppose you never do or you wouldn't get married in the first place, right?"

"Well, your marriage lasted twenty-four years longer than mine did," she said. "So there must've been something between you."

"There was. We were very much in love for most of the marriage."

I could tell that something about the way this conversation was flowing caught my mother off guard. It was his honesty. She wasn't quite sure how to respond, but I detected a change in her voice. The light, seductive purr receded, and she too seemed to become more unguarded and real.

"If you don't mind me asking," she said, "what happened?"

"That's not an easy answer. I guess it never is. Sometimes I wish she'd fallen in love with another man or I'd fallen in love with another woman just so I'd have a shorthand way of explaining what went wrong. Like I said, we were happy for most of the marriage. Our passion cooled a bit over the years, but that's not unusual. I guess things really went wrong after the death of our son, David."

"Oh Lord, I'm sorry. I had no idea," my mother gasped.

My heart tightened in my chest.

"He was a medic in Korea," he continued. "Volunteered before he was even drafted. That's the kind of kid he was. He was killed just two weeks after he got there. It wasn't a combat situation. His ambulance crashed. The driver veered off the road to avoid hitting a Korean girl herding goats. All that time we spent worrying about him getting shot over there, and he died in a simple car accident. We got his first letters home three weeks after we got notice that he had died. It was like hearing a voice from beyond the grave."

"It must've been horrible," my mother said with true sympathy.

"We both took the loss really hard. Some irrational part of us probably blamed each other for what had happened. It's amazing where your mind wanders when you're faced with something like that. He was our only child. It's like half of what we had in common was instantly erased and replaced by this big chunk of shared agony. Just looking at each other reminded us of David. He had her eyes and smile, so looking at her became difficult for me. He had my voice." He broke off and was quiet for a moment. "We held on for a couple of years, but then I think we both just got tired of our misery."

"Do you still talk to her?"

"Sometimes. But less so since the divorce became

final. I still care about her, but there doesn't seem to be much point in pretending anymore. I guess that's why I'm down here trying to reconnect with my brother."

"Did you see him this afternoon?"

"I saw him," he said, "but he didn't see me."

"What do you mean?"

"He runs our family business. Friendly Market on St. Claude."

"Near the Chinese laundry?"

"That's the one," he replied. "I parked my car across the street from the store and just watched him, trying to work up the courage to go inside, but I never did."

I edged forward. Hearing him talk about things I had observed on my spy mission made my spine tingle.

"Why?" she asked.

"I lost my nerve. My brother and I haven't spoken in over twenty years."

"Twenty years!"

"Hard to believe." He nodded.

"I haven't spoken to my sister in eleven years!"

"Maybe they've been hanging around together," he quipped.

"We'd never know, would we?" she said. They both laughed.

"Well, let's see who has the worst sibling story," my mother said. "You go first."

"Oh, come on, I just gave you my broken marriage story. Can't you go first this round?"

"No, the guest always goes first."

"Okay, but I'm going to need another glass of sherry," he said.

She topped off their glasses, and Morgan continued.

"We never had much money growing up," he explained. "My parents started the business and worked themselves to the bone every day of their lives to keep it going."

"It was just you and your brother?"

"Yes. Michael is three years older than me. We were very close when we were growing up. He was a great big brother. Always looking out for me. Our favorite game was playing Treasure Island. I would be the young squire, Jim Hawkins, and he'd be the pirate, Long John Silver. We'd run around the neighborhood with swords cut out of cardboard boxes, looking for treasure. He must've read that book to me fifty times. I really looked up to him. He was bigger and stronger than me. And he was always great at sports and had an easy way with girls, all the things that matter most when you're a kid. Of course, we both worked in the store as soon as we could help out, because my parents couldn't afford to hire anybody.

"I don't remember my parents ever buying anything for themselves. All they seemed to care about was buying us a real education that would give us the opportunities that they never had. When I was ten years old and Michael was thirteen, they had saved enough to send one of us away to private school."

"I think I know where this is going," my mother said.

"I was the obvious choice. I always did a little

better in school, and Michael was older. He was
about to enter high school, and they relied on him
more around the store. So they decided to send me.
Prep school in New Hampshire, then Columbia
undergraduate, and then graduate school. I saw
my family only on school breaks, and then during
college I worked in New York and started coming
home even less. My parents didn't mean to drive a
wedge between us, but I guess it was inevitable. My
brother never went to college and had to stay and
run the business when my parents got too old. I
know he felt that he didn't have any choice."

"Did he ever marry?" my mother asked.

"Yeah. He built a life for himself, got married,
had a couple of kids. But he basically lives the life
of our parents. We both dreamed about escaping
that life. It's irrational, but I know he blames me for
his lost opportunities. There were other issues, of
course. But that's the core of it. Over the years his
bitterness grew and we moved further and further
apart. Every little disagreement blew up into an
argument. We had one final blowout just before the

Second World War. Twenty years later, here we are."

"Well, at least you want to make an effort. If I never saw my sister, Denise, again, it'd be fine by me."

"Okay. Now it's your turn."

"All right," she said. "But I've gotta start with my broken marriage and then go into my sibling rivalry, if you don't mind."

"Bring on the broken marriage," he said.

"It's my own damn fault for falling in love with a drummer in the first place. It's the oldest music business cliché, but I fell right into the trap. Duane was playing with a pop jazz trio around town when we met. I started singing and playing a little piano with them and we weren't half bad, started getting some pretty good bookings. We fell in love, at least I did, and things were going really good for a while. I was still basically a kid, living out my dream of being a girl singer like Helen Forrest or Dinah Shore.

"Then came what seemed like a big break.

Duane got the band a regular gig at a fancy hotel in Baton Rouge. It was gonna be enough money that he could quit his day job and focus on music full-time. We were all going to have to move. My father wouldn't let me go unless Duane married me. And Duane wasn't about to let a silly little wedding ring stand in the way of the band's progress.

"Things went sour in Baton Rouge. My older sister, Denise, was already living there and working the lunch counter at the Woolworth's downtown. Denise was always really girlish-looking. People always thought I was the older sister."

"Were you close growing up?" he asked.

"Oh, sure," she said. "But the rivalry was always there. Even when we were little girls, we fought about who had the prettiest doll, the prettiest dress, the prettiest hair. We were all sticky sweet as pecan pie until a man got in the way. She and Duane took one look at each other and it was like two high-powered magnets. I couldn't have pried those two apart with a crowbar. It took me a while to catch wind of what was going on, but pretty soon I was seeing signs that were too obvious to ignore. We weren't there more than a year when they ran off together to Kansas City."

"I'm sorry," he said.

"I should've known better than to fall for a drummer. And he was trash. Handsome trash, but trash nonetheless." She paused for a moment and then nodded. "But he was fun. He could make me laugh so hard it hurt. He'd do this thing, like a comedy routine with his drums, where he'd make all these funny sound effects as he was telling a story. It was just about the funniest thing you could imagine when he got it going. It was kind of like a Danny Kaye routine, where he got all worked up till his hair started flying everywhere and his face turned red. He did all sorts of imitations, too: Edward G. Robinson, Cary Grant. He was a real performer."

That part of the story was brand-new to me. I had absolutely no idea that my father had a sense of humor or that he could imitate movie stars or that he ever made my mother laugh. Suddenly I wanted to hear more good things about him, to fill in some of the dark empty spaces he always held in my mind.

"So he left you alone with Louise?"

"He ran out on us just after she was born."

"Poor kid," he said.

"I haven't heard from either of them since May 12, 1948. Just one week after Louise arrived."

"I'll never understand how people can abandon their babies," he said sadly.

Tears silently ran down my face and into my mouth. I wiped my eyes and nose with the back of my hand, choking back the sobs. I had heard my mother tell the story of my father's abandonment in various forms over the years and it had never made me cry. I had never shed any tears for my lost father. It never really occurred to me to miss him. First of all, I never knew him, so there was really nothing to miss. Occasionally, kids around the neighborhood would tease me about not having a daddy, but that just made me mad, not sad. The other reason I never thought to miss him was that until that night, my mother had never said even the most vaguely positive thing about him. Part of me felt bad for my mother for the first time in a long time. Not many people made her laugh these days.

Yet I think what made me so upset was the fact that Morgan was hearing the story and pitying me.

"We always had music in common," she continued. "That boy could really play."

"Do you still play?" He nodded to the piano.

"Just here and there."

"I'd love to hear something."

"Oh, stop," she said.

"Please. I am the guest making a request."

My mother almost never played the piano anymore. Every once in a while I'd hear her singing along to the radio, but that was it. From what I could tell, she did have a nice voice.

"Well, my pipes are pretty rusty," she said as she moved to the piano. "So be kind."

"I'm an easy audience," he assured her.

"My signature song was 'Do You Know What It Means to Miss New Orleans' by Alter and DeLange.

We always had to play the songs with local flavor for the tourists."

Ricky Nelson had just released a version of the song, and it was getting played on local radio, but I'd never heard my mother's arrangement. She played it as an ultra-slow blues number. Her voice surprised me. It was fragile and girlish, but also a little rough around the edges. Her version communicated a sense of longing that Ricky Nelson's didn't. It wasn't until I heard Billie Holiday's recording of the song that I discovered the origin of my mother's interpretation. She seemed to be able to give each word meaning, as if she were singing about her own longing for a real man.

> *Do you know what it means to miss*
> *   New Orleans*
> *And miss it each night and day*
> *I know I'm not wrong . . . the feeling's*
> *   getting stronger*
> *The longer I stay away*

Miss the moss-covered vines . . . tall
sugar pines
Where mockingbirds used to sing
And I'd like to see that lazy
Mississippi . . .
Hurrying into spring

The moonlight on the bayou. . . .
A Creole tune . . . that fills the air
I dream . . . about magnolias in
bloom . . .
and I'm wishin' I was there

Do you know what it means to miss
New Orleans
When that's where you left your heart
And there's one thing more . . . I miss
the one I care for
More than I miss New Orleans

She finished with a little piano flourish and
Morgan applauded.

"Bravo!" he said. "That was wonderful."

"Well, I'm no Peggy Lee."

"Peggy doesn't sing with half the feeling you've got."

"Oh, please."

"I mean it."

"Flattery will get you everywhere," my mother said, the seductive purr returning to her voice. Morgan coughed, and there was an uncomfortable beat of silence. At this point I was waiting for my mother to pull out one of her clinchers. If she was trying to seduce a shy man, she had a number of lines she used to snare him. Before she had the chance, Morgan said something completely unexpected.

"Would you allow me to take you to dinner tomorrow night?"

"Dinner?" my mother said.

"Yes," he said. "I've never been to Commander's Palace, and I've always wanted to try it."

This took my mother and me completely by surprise. The men she was used to consorting with almost never invited her to dine. And even if they did, Commander's Palace was way out of their league. Tucked away in the Garden District, Commander's Palace was considered the very finest restaurant in all of New Orleans. The restaurant had played host to everyone from Jefferson Davis to Mark Twain to Elvis Presley. A meal there would cost at least a week's worth of our income. I know my mother had always yearned to go there. After shaking off the shock, she managed to reply.

"I'd be delighted."

"Great. We'll plan on six thirty?"

"That'd be fine," she said.

"I'd better hit the sack. I've got an early break-fast. But I want to thank you for a most lovely evening."

"It was my pleasure."

I stuck my head back down into the heating duct just in time to see Morgan and my mother rise.

"Good night, Pauline." He gave her a gentle kiss on the hand, just like the one he gave me.

"Good night, Morgan," she said.

He turned to walk upstairs. My mother stood in place for a moment, letting it all sink in. I heard Morgan's footsteps on the top of the stairs before I remembered that I needed to replace the grate and get out of there.

CHAPTER 10

Now, as I mentioned earlier, the blood tended to rush to my head whenever I'd lower it down into the heating duct. I hurriedly pushed the grate back into place, but as soon as I tried to stand up, I knew something was wrong. The walls seemed to fold down on top of me, and my stomach and head felt like they were twisting in opposite directions. Then my knees turned to jelly and I blacked out, just like that. I'd never fainted before, so I had no idea what was happening at the time.

When I opened my eyes again, I didn't have any sense of how much time had passed. All I knew was

that I was lying on the floor of the second-story
bathroom with my mother and Morgan huddled
over me.

Then I saw the blood on the front of my dress.
Earlier that afternoon I had prayed to the Lord for
puberty to overtake me so that I could sprout breasts
to rival my mother's. As I lay on the bathroom floor,
my heart filled with paralyzing dread: I realized
that my desperate prayer had been answered in the
most horrible way possible: I had gotten my period.

I didn't know much about menstruation, but
what I did know I didn't like one bit. My mother
had never had a "birds and the bees" talk with me,
so most of what I knew came from Jez Robidoux,
who maintained that during your period you peed
blood instead of urine. "Why do girls make blood
instead of boys?" I asked.

"I don't know," she replied, and then added:
"There's all sorts of stuff that's different between
boys and girls, right? If you start asking those questions, why not ask why girls have vaginas in the first
place instead of a penis? Did you ever think about

that? Why don't you have a penis, Louise?" It was hard for me to argue with that logic.

Just a few hours earlier I had prayed for puberty to grow breasts; now here I was praying for a miraculous reversal to dam the menstrual river.

As my eyes blinked open, I noticed that Morgan looked concerned. My mother looked concerned too, but also more than slightly annoyed.

"She's coming to," he said.

"Thank the Lord," my mother replied.

"I guess she fainted."

"Louise, honey," she asked, "are you all right?

My mother helped pull me up to a sitting position.

"Sugar, can you hear me?"

I nodded.

"Are you okay?" Morgan asked.

"I think so," I said.

"You gave your nose and lips a pretty good whack," he said. "You must've fainted and hit the edge of the toilet on the way down."

My nose and lips! That's when I first felt the

hotness running over my lips and down my chin. It wasn't my period! The blood had splattered the front of my dress from my nose! Rejoice! I felt my mind rush to thank the Lord but then stopped myself short, not wishing to risk bringing God into my personal life any more that day. I ran my tongue over my lips and felt a small opening oozing blood.

"It doesn't look like your nose is broken," Morgan said.

I slowly stood up and discovered my knees were solid again.

"I'll get her cleaned up," my mother said to Morgan. "Please go to bed—you've been more than kind."

"All right," he said. "Good night, ladies."

He exited as my mother wet a washcloth and began to wipe down my face and neck. She let a moment pass to make sure Morgan was out of earshot, and then she interrogated me in a hushed rasp.

"And what were you doing in here at such a late hour?" she asked.

"Going to the bathroom," I said.

"Still wearing your dinner dress? You should've been in your nightgown and asleep an hour ago."

I didn't respond.

She rubbed the bottom of my neck hard with the washcloth, all pretense of tenderness gone.

"I can't have you running around the house like a wild animal at all hours of the night. What do you think our guests think of that?"

"I don't know."

"I'll tell you what they think, that I'm a bad mother who raised a disrespectful swamp rat of a child. I will not have you making me look bad in front of guests, Louise, do you understand? I want you to be in bed at a proper hour. You hear?"

I nodded.

She tossed the bloody washcloth into the sink.

"Sometimes I don't know how I put up with you," she said. "And will you look at that dress? You probably ruined it."

She tugged the dress off over my head.

"Go downstairs and soak this in some water and

Ivory flakes before the blood dries."

I looked down at myself, naked save for a pair of old panties.

"Go on," she said. "I paid good money for that thing."

My mother flung the dress at me and walked out. I grabbed my pink cotton robe from a hook on the back of the door, slipped it on, and then went downstairs to wash the dress.

CHAPTER 11

The next morning I slept until seven thirty and cursed myself. I had fully intended to follow Morgan to his morning rendezvous, but I was so tired from my late night of surveillance, fainting, bleeding, and washing that I just couldn't wake myself up. I finally stirred at the sound of Mr. Landroux's bell ringing for breakfast, a bedpan change, or both.

My mother had the enviable ability to sleep through nearly any noise. Part of this skill must be attributed to the lime juleps, which nicely dulled most of her senses when she slept. Yet that morning she was already awake when Mr. Landroux started ringing. She added a shrill vocal to accompany the bell.

"Louise! Louise!" she called. "Can't you hear the bell?"

I got up and pulled on some clothes. As I trudged out into the hallway toward the stairs, my mother emerged from her room. To my surprise she was already dressed in her powder-blue dress with the heart print, and her hair was neatly arranged with a matching blue bow. She leaned one hand on the railing of the stairwell and pulled on a blue patent leather pump.

"After you're done with Mr. Landroux, make sure you make a fresh pitcher of lemonade," she said. "And sweep out the front hall before Mr. Miller returns in the afternoon."

"Why are you going so early?" I asked.

"Don't you remember? It's Monday."

"Yeah, but you don't usually go until eight thirty . . ."

"I've got three letters for you, Louise: C-B-S."

A rumor had circulated at the end of the previous

week that CBS News was sending down a television crew to do a story about the Cheerleaders. All the ladies were hoping to get on TV. My mother planned to arrive extra early to insure that she had the best position for the camera.

She pulled on her other pump and headed downstairs. She called back to me as she rushed out the front door.

"If Mr. Miller comes back, you just be sure to tend to him properly."

The bell rang again, more insistently.

CHAPTER 12

After cleaning Mr. Landroux's bedpan and serving him a breakfast of oatmeal, coffee, and tomato juice, I went back downstairs to clean Morgan's room. I took great care making up his room. I made sure his hospital corners were extra tight on the bed, and I puffed up his pillow so it looked just right. I laid out fresh towels, careful to choose the ones with the fewest rips and stains. I polished the mirror over the dresser, making sure not to leave any stray fingerprints along the way.

With my chores complete, I slipped back into spy mode and very carefully searched through

Morgan's possessions. Typically, I'd just start rifling through everything without giving it a thought, but with Morgan I hesitated. I almost never felt any pangs of guilt about violating the privacy of our guests. Oh, I knew I was doing something wrong. But I never felt as if it was seriously wrong, just a little bit wrong. It's not as if I was going to tell anyone if I found anything interesting. Of course, my mother or Charlotte would have severely punished me if they knew about my searches. And I didn't have any friends I trusted enough to share vital information like that with, even Jez.

Over the years I did make some notable discoveries. All were dutifully recorded in my Spy Log with the following information: date, guest's name, a brief description of the guest, and a description of the key object.

June 23, 1958: J. Agostino. Salesman from Indiana. Set of 25 jars with preserved animal babies in formaldehyde, including frogs, a baby chick, and a bat.

April 14, 1959: The Petersons. Old couple
from Mississippi. The books *Sexual Behavior
in the Human Male* and *Sexual Behavior in the
Human Female* by Dr. Alfred Kinsey. No
pictures.

May 24, 1959: M. Smith. Trucker from
Alabama. One Colt revolver wrapped in a
red bandanna and a box of bullets.

January 16, 1960: S. Hermanson. Marine on
leave. Photos of naked men posing on the
beach.

March 29, 1960: J & J Johnson. Country boys.
Six jugs of moonshine and $75 in rolled
quarters, dimes, and nickels.

My affection and respect for Morgan gave me a
moment's pause before I completely violated his privacy. But it was really only a moment. I took my
surveillance of Morgan so seriously that I retrieved

my Spy Log to record everything I found, not wanting to risk any detail to faulty memory. He had
unpacked his suitcase and put his clothes in the
dresser. I went through each item, recorded it in my
log, and carefully put everything back exactly how I
found it.

5 crew-neck T-shirts

6 pairs of socks, four black, two brown

4 button-down shirts with a label from a store
    called Monty's for Men, New York

6 pairs of white boxer shorts

2 pairs of slacks, one brown, one beige

1 blue blazer, also from Monty's for Men, New
    York

Nothing out of the ordinary there. His toilet kit
also yielded very little of interest. Although he did
use some very pleasant-smelling brand of aftershave
and talc called Pinaud Clubman. The label read
"World Famous Since 1810." I unscrewed the cap of
the aftershave and took a deep sniff—it was the

source of the faintly sweet but masculine scent that I had noticed at dinner.

Although I was usually disappointed to find nothing of interest in a guest's room, with Morgan I was relieved. I didn't want to have my image of him dimmed by some hidden vice tucked away in his underwear drawer. In truth I was searching in the hopes of not finding anything incriminating.

I completed my accounting of his possessions and was returning everything to exactly where it was when I noticed a small leather briefcase beside the door. Of course I couldn't let something like that elude my investigation. The first thing I pulled out of the case was an unopened pack of Lucky Strikes. Next I retrieved a 257-page manuscript of a book called *Landing the Job: Tips for Recent Graduates*, by Alice Timmons. I flipped through the pages and read through some of what I assumed were Morgan's comments written in blue ink along the margins.

Page 71—"Let's move the résumé section earlier. Maybe Chapter 3?"

Page 128—"Great section on what not to
wear. Line about the purple tie made me
laugh out loud."

Page 232—"More sample interview
questions would be useful. Something about
long-term goals, etc."

None of the notes made much sense without
really knowing the context, but I assumed they were
all brilliant and helpful. Insane jealousy swept over
me at the thought of Alice Timmons getting to
work with Morgan. Did this girl realize how lucky
she was?

The next item I retrieved was a small newspaper. I was just going to put it aside when the name
flashed before my eyes and I froze. A chill ran
through my entire body as the words sank in.

DAILY WORKER

I instinctively dropped the paper like a hot coal
and stared in horror. This was the paper of record of

Communist conspirators and enemies of all things good. Pornography, guns, moonshine—none of those hit me with the same shock of revulsion as was caused by Morgan's copy of the *Daily Worker*. For a moment I was afraid to touch it. In my universe Communists ranked neck and neck with Satan on the chart of evildoers. Was Morgan one of *them*?

I dumped out the rest of the briefcase, fearful I'd find a cache of microfilm, a dagger with the Soviet hammer and sickle emblazoned on the handle, or a secret transmitting device to communicate with the Kremlin. But there was nothing else in the bag save a Zippo lighter and a pack of Juicy Fruit gum. My mind raced in the opposite direction, hoping to absolve Morgan of this ugly suspicion. He must work for the FBI, I assured myself, and he was merely researching the enemy. Yes . . . he must be some sort of government agent. That must be it.

I turned my full attention to the paper. The front-page headline read "Garment Strike Looms." I flipped through the entire contents, scanning the articles, all of which concerned the oppression of workers and other abuses by bosses and corporations. Nothing really penetrated until I got to the very last page, the sports section, where Morgan's name jumped out at me from the byline of an editorial column.

Boston Still a Racist Stronghold

By M. I. Miller, Sports Editor

Imagine an outfield with both Ted Williams and Willie Mays. Sounds like a fantasy, right? That fantasy could have been a reality. The Boston Red Sox had the opportunity to sign Willie in 1949 and perhaps build the greatest baseball dynasty of the 1950s. The Red Sox sent a scout to look at the young Say Hey Kid, but the game was delayed by rain. The scout left, deciding it wasn't worth waiting to check out a Negro ballplayer, because they probably

*wouldn't sign him anyway. The racism
of the Red Sox management was a boon
to New York Giants fans like me, but a
disgrace to baseball.*

My heart sank. M. I. Miller was a Giants fan.
Morgan did not work for the FBI. He was one of
them. Worse still, he wasn't just one of them: He
was an editor, a person of authority on the *Daily
Worker*.

Some tiny alarm bell went off in my head, telling
me that I should go to William Frantz Elementary
School right away. At the Citizens' Council meetings the speakers blamed the Communists for incit-
ing the Negroes. Would I find Morgan holding a
sign or passing out pamphlets or just generally incit-
ing civil unrest? I stuffed everything back into the
bag and ran to find out.

CHAPTER 13

It's important to remember that the Cheerleaders weren't some crazy fringe group. Literally everyone I knew supported segregation. Nearly every elected official in the state of Louisiana had marshaled all available power to block integration. In the months leading up to the beginning of the school year, the state legislature had passed more than two dozen new anti-integration laws. Governor Jimmie H. Davis himself swore he'd go to jail before he'd let Negro kids into a white school.

To my mind it seemed as if the only white person in the entire state of Louisiana who supported school integration was U.S. District Court Judge J. Skelly Wright. I heard Judge Wright called every nasty name in the book, from "nigger lover" to "Communist spy" to plain old "nut job." Kids in the neighborhood referred to him as "Go-to-Helly Wright" or "Old Smelly Skelly" or simply "Judge Skelly Wrong." Whatever he was, Judge Wright seemed to be determined as a mule to let school integration proceed.

Since every single white parent had pulled their children out of my school, Ruby Bridges was the sole student in the building at the beginning. Eventually a few white parents broke the boycott, but in those first few months it was never more than a handful. And no one ever dared to join Ruby Bridges's class. She was taught by a single teacher all by herself for the entire year. None of the regular teachers at Frantz would go near her, so Ruby was assigned to someone new to the school system who was an outsider. Rumor had it that the teacher herself was a Northern agitator, specifically planted by the N.A.A.C.P. I heard some of the ladies gossip that this teacher was everything from a Communist to a beatnik to a nymphomaniac who specifically liked to have sexual relations with black men.

Since November, big crowds had gathered in front of the building two times a day every week-day—once in the morning when school began and once in the afternoon when school let out. Typically, the crowd in front of the school consisted of the following groups in varying numbers.

The Cheerleaders
Rednecks and good old boys (like Royce Burke)
Local police officers
FBI agents
Journalists
High school boys
Random spectators
Neighborhood kids

I rode my bike down North Galvez, and the crowd grew thicker and thicker as I neared the school. I arrived on the scene just before eight thirty

A.M. and stowed my bike between two parked cars near the corner of Alvar Street. I scanned the crowd and breathed a small sigh of relief when I didn't spot Morgan or his Chevy Bel Air anywhere in the vicinity. I passed along the fringes of the crowd, careful to go unnoticed.

Right away I could tell that the CBS television crew had not shown up, because my mother stood toward the back of the group of Cheerleaders, smoking a cigarette with her friend Nitty Babcock. Approximately thirty ladies gathered that day, and no one jockeyed to be at the front of the pack.

Royce Burke and a few of his friends leaned against a pickup truck nearby, eyeballing everything that went on. There was a tremendous amount of eyeballing going on at all times. Whenever an unfamiliar face or vehicle arrived on the scene, everyone took note. FBI agents milled around in their sharp blue or gray suits, taking down license plate numbers and descriptions of suspicious-looking characters in little black notebooks. I wasn't the only one in my neighborhood who kept a Spy Log.

The Cheerleaders always gathered at the same spot on the sidewalk beside the school's main entrance. John Steinbeck later described them as a pack of satanic dogs. But the truth is they were not dogs, satanic or otherwise. They were just a normal-looking bunch of ladies. If you didn't know any better, you'd think they were gathered for a church bake sale or a PTA meeting. A couple of them might be described as naturally mean-looking. Bea Williams had deep lines in her forehead and down the side of her cheeks, which made her look cross all the time, and Jeanette LeFevre had a pinched face and a shrill voice. But other than those two they were an extremely average-looking bunch, except for my mother, who most people said was beautiful.

Most of the Cheerleaders dressed plainly compared to my mother, but almost all of them dressed decently. There were a few housecoats in the group, and several wore their hair in curlers under head kerchiefs in the morning (something my mother would never do in public). Some commentators noted that the fact that they wore their hair in curlers was a sign the Cheerleaders were low class. In truth, no one in the Ninth Ward could really be described as high class, and it was probably unfair to criticize them for wearing curlers in the early morning. Many of the ladies worked at jobs, so they didn't have much time to take care of themselves before they had to stage their daily protest. When else could they curl their hair?

Several women held signs on wooden sticks that read WE *WANT* SEGREGATION, GOD BLESS JIMMIE DAVIS, and READ YOUR BIBLE — INTEGRATION IS WRONG! Others carried light wooden crosses or small Confederate battle flags. Bea Williams frequently brought a Negro baby doll in a tiny wooden coffin that she'd prop up on the sidewalk so Ruby Bridges could see it as she walked up.

The group's leader, Ada Munson, always stood at the front and led the chant: "Two, four, six, eight, We don't want to integrate!" Every morning the ladies brought articles from local newspapers in which they were mentioned. They'd begin the day by reading the articles aloud like a bunch of actresses poring over reviews of a stage performance.

On that morning Ada Munson held a copy of the *Jackson Daily News*, a newspaper from Mississippi featuring an article with the headline "Woman Throws Egg." She read highlights aloud to the group. "A Negro truck driver stopped at a traffic light in front of the William Frantz School in New Orleans on Friday, and a white woman threw an egg at him." A few of the ladies laughed. "The egg missed the Negro's head and smashed against the roof of the cab. The Negro man glared and drove away. The egg thrower was one of the Cheerleaders, Mrs. Antoinette Lawrence." A few of the ladies gave a small round of applause for Antoinette, a petite brunette who giggled, gave a little wave, and said, "Oh, stop." Ada Munson continued reading. "'I don't think the niggers are equal to whites,' said Mrs. Lawrence. 'Their heads are too hard to learn what our children can. We are going to win this fight. Let them niggers try to keep coming. I've got plenty of eggs.'"

My mother stood in the back of the group, not really listening. I overheard a snippet of her conversation with Nitty Babcock.

"And I'll give you just one guess where he's taking me for dinner tonight," my mother said.

"Hell, I don't know, Pauline, just tell me," Nitty replied.

"It's no fun if you don't guess."

"Pauline, you are acting like a twelve-year-old child. Just spit it out."

My mother allowed for a dramatic pause and then blurted it out.

"Commander's Palace."

"You're lying." Nitty giggled.

"Honest," my mother replied, holding up her hand as if swearing an oath.

"I've always wanted to go dere."

"Don't think I haven't."

"What are you gonna wear, sweetheart?"

"That is the sixty-four-thousand-dollar question. I couldn't sleep a wink last night trying to decide between my little blue cocktail dress and my orange number with the floral print. You know, the one that has the nice sloping neckline."

"You've gotta go wid da cocktail dress."

"You think so?"

"Oh, yeah. It's real nice."

"I'll bring the bag with the baby pearls along the handle."

"That's perfect. Do you think he's really met John Steinbeck?"

"He hasn't just met him," my mother corrected. "He's his friend, for Christ's sake. They're practically best friends. He's had dinner at the man's house with Mrs. Steinbeck on many occasions, just like regular people."

"Lord, I wonder what people like dat say to each other."

"Why, they're just people, Nitty. He had a regular conversation with me, just like he was talking to anyone. I mean, he's obviously more refined than most people around here, but it's not like he's from Mars or something."

"How you gonna do your hair?"

"I haven't a clue. I was just starting to go through my magazine collection this morning to get some new ideas when I had to rush on down here like a fool. I just hope Corrine can come up with something sophisticated for me. Last time I asked for 'sophisticated,' she made me look like Mamie Eisenhower. I swear I came out of there looking like a cocker spaniel . . ."

Suddenly my mother stopped talking as something caught her eye in the distance. I followed her gaze to see Morgan's Bel Air pull to a stop and park not too far down the street.

CHAPTER 14

Morgan got out of his car, locked the door, put on a pair of sunglasses, and walked toward the front of the school. At first I thought he might just walk up the front steps and go inside. Instead he took a position on the sidewalk directly across from the Cheerleaders and gazed around at the crowd. His face revealed nothing; he just seemed to be observing. I'm not sure why, but my mother instinctively drew back and quickly slipped on a pair of sunglasses.

Outsiders always drew everyone's attention, and

Morgan was no exception. Royce Burke nudged one of his friends with an elbow and gestured toward Morgan with his chin. They whispered to each other. Two FBI men also took notice of Morgan and made notations in their little black books. A third FBI man wrote down the number of Morgan's license plate.

My mother silently watched him. Nitty noticed my mother's unsettled expression.

"Pauline, what's wrong?" she asked.

"N-nothing," my mother stammered.

Just at that moment the crowd noise swelled as a black Pontiac sedan carrying Ruby Bridges pulled up in front of the school. Morgan and everyone else turned their attention to the car. The Cheerleaders brandished their signs and, like a mad conductor, Ada Munson started to lead the furious chanting.

> *Two, four, six, eight.*
> *We don't want to integrate!*
> *Two, four, six, eight.*
> *We don't want to integrate!*

Four tall federal marshals wearing white armbands took up positions beside the back door of the car, and six-year-old Ruby Bridges emerged from inside. She was a little black speck of a thing dressed in a blindingly white cotton dress. I could never understand why they let her wear those white dresses. With everyone so upset about her brown skin, it just made her skin look that much darker.

Once all four men were in position around her, the group moved toward the school in unison. The crowd grew louder and more unruly the closer she got to the building. I was always amazed at how Ruby managed to maintain her composure. She never cried or even flinched. She just walked right into the school beside her bodyguards and didn't give any indication that she heard or saw all the commotion swirling around her. How do you train yourself not to turn around when everyone's screaming at you? Maybe she was partially deaf, I reasoned.

At the time I wondered how and why she got

picked to be the sole Negro student at our school. I assumed she must've been the unluckiest little Negro girl on the planet. I later learned that the plan to integrate the New Orleans public schools was very carefully orchestrated to minimize public outrage. The Ninth Ward was chosen because it had political advantages for the pro-integration forces. Because our neighborhood was one of the poorest sections of town, it consisted of citizens with the least political clout and therefore the least ability to fight the decision to integrate. The Cheerleaders were well aware of this fact. I had heard my mother grumbling, "Of course they wouldn't dare integrate a school in one of the uptown wards."

The integration plan called for students to enter the first grade, and then new first graders would be added each year until the entire school system was integrated. Only girls were selected in the first year, to stave off hysteria that the Negro boys might try to kiss the white girls (or worse). In an effort to block or slow down the integration process, the state insisted that Negro children take an extremely difficult entrance exam to qualify to go to a white school. Ruby Bridges was one of the few who passed.

News reports at the time were too polite to record the ugliest moments outside William Frantz. And it did get ugly. High school boys snarled at her, "Here, nigger, nigger, nigger. Here, nigger, nigger, nigger," like they were calling out to a cat. One of Royce Burke's cohorts, Clem Deneen, liked to throw paper bags filled with dog poop at her. Royce Burke favored verbal threats. "Tell your mama and daddy we're throwing a party for dem," he'd say. "A lynching party."

Perhaps the most hateful piece of heckling came from the relatively soft voice of Antoinette Lawrence. Every single morning she would lean in close as Ruby passed by and whisper death threats at her, saying she was going to poison her food. I later learned that because of Antoinette's threats, Ruby had secretly skipped lunch every day for more than a month. Her teacher eventually found out what was going on when she discovered a huge stash of uneaten sandwiches rotting in a cabinet in the back of the classroom.

Typically, my mother was just one of the pack, a rank-and-file Cheerleader. She didn't have a unique brand of taunting. She'd usually just join in with whatever chorus Ada would lead. She never carried a sign, cross, or flag. I think she avoided these props because she feared they'd take attention away from one of her matching parasols, handbags, or bracelets. But she always participated. I'd seen her throw eggs and tomatoes and cheer with the same intensity as the others, but not on this day. On this day she just stood in the back with her eyes locked on Morgan.

Ruby and her escorts made their way up the steps amid the chants, threats, and thrown objects. Morgan just watched with a hard expression on his face. After one final crescendo of howls, the front door of the school closed and they were inside the building.

CHAPTER 15

The morning show on North Galvez did not end once Ruby Bridges was inside the school. By December there was a handful of white students back at William Frantz Elementary. These kids were not granted federal bodyguards, so their parents had to walk them to school every day themselves. As it turned out, the white kids may have needed more protection than the Negroes. The ugliest displays of hate were reserved for the white parents who dared to cross the picket lines. To the Cheerleaders, good old boys, and rednecks, nothing was worse than a race traitor. Ada Munson put it this way: "Da niggers are too stupid to know any better. Dey're just being manipulated. But if you're white, you ain't got no excuses."

For the most part, the few parents who sent their kids were already considered outsiders in some regard. Herman and Maria Letterman sent their daughter Sophia. But Mrs. Letterman was from Spain, so she was not considered one hundred percent American, despite being a fully naturalized U.S. citizen. Her foreign birth explained her confused racial attitudes. The Reverend and Mrs. Eleanor Jenks sent their son, Timothy. At his church the Reverend Jenks had been preaching about how the Bible taught us to be color-blind and that Jesus would definitely have been in favor of integration. Everyone thought he had a perverted reading of Scripture, and he had lost many of his congregants. Father Bryson, one of the local Catholic priests, also used his pulpit to preach in favor of desegregating the schools. "Easy enough for a priest to say," my mother sneered. "They never have kids of their own to worry about."

Morgan did not stay to watch any more of the show. After Ruby Bridges entered the building, he returned to his car. He arrived to discover Royce Burke and Clem Deneen leaning against the driver's-side door of his Bel Air with their arms folded. Most outsiders and tourists simply avoided the area like it was a war zone. Curious observers who wanted to catch a glimpse of the spectacle were usually careful to be as discreet as possible. For instance, when Mr. John Steinbeck paid a visit to watch the Cheerleaders, he disguised himself as a tourist from Liverpool, England, for fear of being accosted by the crowd if they suspected he was a fellow American. Morgan had prepared no such ruse. When he approached his car, Royce and Clem made no move to clear out of the way. They straightened up and tightened their arms across their chests.

"Excuse me," Morgan said.

"You want us to move?" Royce asked.

"Yes."

"Now?" Clem responded.

"Yes," Morgan replied. "Now."

"We're happy to oblige you, sir."

"No problem at all," Clem nodded.

Clem and Royce switched places so that they were still blocking the door. They giggled like they were the cleverest duo this side of Abbott and Costello. Morgan didn't laugh. My mother watched from the back of the pack of Cheerleaders.

"Please move," Morgan said firmly.

"Why you leaving?" Royce asked. "Don't you want to see da whole show?"

"I've seen enough, thank you."

"You drove all da way down here from New York and dat's all you're gonna stay for? Dat's a shame, ain't it, Clem?"

"A dirty shame." Clem nodded.

"I'll ask you again," Morgan said. "Please move out of my way."

"*Please* move. We got ourselves a real gentleman, Clem."

"Where you from, boy?" Clem asked.

"New Orleans, if you must know."

"Well, your car and your voice sound like dey're

from *Jew* York . . . I mean, New York City," Royce replied.

"I was born here," Morgan answered.

"Oh, really," said Royce. "Den I'm sure you understand da way we like things down here, right?"

Morgan stared at him for a long moment and then sighed. "Are you going to let me get into my car?"

"Why, sure," said Royce.

Royce and Clem separated just enough to expose the handle of the car door. Morgan hesitated but then stepped forward with his key. He placed the key in the door and unlocked it. He turned the handle, but because Clem and Royce were still in the way, he couldn't really open it.

"Excuse me," Morgan said.

Clem refused to budge.

"I said excuse me," he said more firmly. Morgan opened the door so it brushed the back of Clem's legs ever so slightly.

"What da hell are you doing, boy?" Clem snarled.

"I believe he's getting physical with you, Clem."

"I believe you're right," Clem replied.

"Please just let me—" But before Morgan could complete his sentence, Clem gave him a quick, hard elbow in the ribs. Morgan gasped but then reacted quickly by pushing Clem, who lost his footing and stumbled back. Royce leaped forward and grabbed Morgan, pinning his arms behind his back. A few of the other good old boys and two local police officers took notice and gathered around the three men in a circle. The police officers wore small grins and made no move to break up the action.

"All right!"

"Let him have it, boys!"

"Show him some tooth, Royce!"

Real fistfights look kind of silly and strange when you see them up close. In movies and television shows, fights usually look orderly. In a typical Western or gangster picture one man punches another man, who falls back and then retaliates with his own punch. But when you really see grown men fighting, it looks sloppy, ugly, and unpredictable.

While Royce struggled to hold Morgan's arms twisted behind his back, Morgan kicked and flailed with his feet to keep Clem at a distance. Clem roared forward and managed to punch Morgan hard in the stomach. Morgan winced and his knees bent, but he didn't fall. Part of me wanted to rush forward and throw myself in front of Morgan to protect him. Another part of me wanted to grab the police officers and shake them for not breaking things up. Still another part of me longed to just run away as fast and as far as I could. But the biggest part of me just froze up with a fear so powerful, I don't think I could've willed my body to move at all. My eyes darted over to my mother, who also seemed to be frozen in place, staring in paralyzed disbelief.

Clem landed a quick punch to Morgan's gut that brought him down on one knee. He coughed and doubled over. The crowd of onlookers cheered their approval. Clem reared back to give him a kick in the face. Just before the blow landed, Morgan lunged forward and grabbed at Clem's leg. He managed to catch and latch onto a piece of Clem's ankle. Clem tumbled over and Morgan twisted on top of him. Both men rolled on the ground. Clem pressed Morgan's face against the pavement. Royce jumped on top of them and punched Morgan a couple of times on the back before a few more police rushed over. A big crowd had gathered, hooting and cheering louder. Even the local police couldn't ignore what had now turned into such an obvious public disturbance. Four new police officers came forward and separated the men.

"All right boys, let's break it up," said a police sergeant as he pulled them apart.

The three men got back on their feet and stared at one another. The crowd clapped and egged on Royce and Clem. Morgan dusted himself off. A small trickle of blood ran down from the corner of his mouth, which he wiped with the back of his hand. A few pebbles were embedded in the side of his cheek and on his forehead from when Clem had pressed his face against the ground. The inside of his mouth must have been bleeding, because I saw his front teeth stained pink as he ran his tongue over them to make sure they were still in place.

"What da hell is going on here?" the sergeant asked.

"I'm just trying to get into my car," Morgan replied.

"He was starting trouble, Officer," Royce countered. "Clem and I was just standing here, and he gave Clem a shove."

Some of the good old boys nodded and shouted their agreement.

"Dat's right."

"He did!"

"Uh-huh."

"A man's gotta be able to defend himself, right, Sarge?" Clem added.

More of the good old boys chimed in with their assent.

"Dat's right."

"Can't let someone just shove you."

"Got dat right!"

"What da hell's da world coming to?" Royce asked. "We got niggers in da schools and New

Yorkers coming down thinking dey can push people around."

"It ain't right."

"No sir, it ain't."

The sergeant stared at Morgan.

"That's not the way it happened," Morgan said plainly.

The crowd roared its disapproval. The police sergeant pointed at Morgan and jerked his thumb toward the street.

"Just get outa here. I don't want to see you round here again. You hear?"

Morgan didn't reply. He just walked toward his car. The good old boys laughed and whistled. Royce and Clem still stood in his path. After a moment's pause they parted and let Morgan pass. Morgan got into the car and started the engine. Royce momentarily stepped in front of the car.

He stared at Morgan and smiled. "I'm watching you."

Royce stepped aside. Morgan wrenched the car into gear and pulled away. He never saw me or my mother, but both of us had our eyes locked on him as the Bel Air drove away down North Galvez. The retreating car was followed by hoots, whistles, and catcalls.

"Stay da hell away!"

"Go back to New York!"

"Nigger lover!"

"Watch your back, boy!"

The noise of the crowd swelled again, and everyone seemed to tighten back into position around the school. Down the sidewalk Herman Letterman was walking toward the entrance, clutching his ten-year-old daughter, Sophia, around the shoulders. Unlike Ruby Bridges, Sophia Letterman looked scared out of her wits. Her eyes darted around at the crowd, and she clutched the edge of her father's jacket like it was her only lifeline. Mr. Letterman wore a tight frown of determination and kept his eyes on the school entrance. Some of the onlookers threw tomatoes, while others bombarded them with words.

"Race traitors!"

"Nigger lovers!"

"Take your foreign whore of a wife and go back to her country!"

A tomato struck Herman Letterman in the back of the neck, and the crowd roared with laughter. Mr. Letterman didn't react. He hurried his daughter up the stairs. Ada Munson led another furious chorus.

> *Two, four, six, eight,*
> *We don't want to integrate!*

My mother wasn't paying attention to the school anymore. She stared off into the distance, where Morgan's car had disappeared. I ran to get my bike, hoping I'd be able to catch up with him.

CHAPTER 16

Mr. John Steinbeck's visit to William Frantz Elementary School left him stunned and disgusted by what he witnessed. He questioned the very humanity of the Cheerleaders and expressed complete dismay at the complicity of the community at large. How could so many people watch an innocent child be bombarded with such violent hatred? Who was worse, the protestors attacking the child or the scores of silent witnesses who allowed it to happen?

Segregation was something everyone in our neighborhood just took for granted. If you had asked your average Ninth Warder at the time if there should be segregated schools, it would've been like asking "Should the sky be blue?" In the Middle Ages everyone just assumed the world was flat—they didn't have any good reason to think otherwise. Then Copernicus came along with this new way of looking at things. I'd bet that Copernicus's neighbors probably thought he was a complete nut job. But it's not as if he was going to try to push people over the edge of the world to prove he was right. It was just a theoretical idea that didn't put any direct responsibility or pressure on ordinary people. Integration was also a theoretical idea, but it was a theoretical idea that people in the Ninth Ward were being asked to put into action. For my mother, the idea of sending a child into an integrated school was just as crazy as taking a walk off the edge of the flat Earth.

I'd love to be able to say that deep in my thirteen-year-old heart I believed in integration and hated my mother for what she was doing. But the fact of the matter is I never really gave it a thought, except to resent the fact that my mother never took any interest in my education until the news reporters and photographers started showing up outside the front entrance of the school. Sure I felt bad for Ruby Bridges. I really did. But it never occurred to me that my mother and the others were wrong. I just felt sorry that Ruby was being manipulated by her parents, the N.A.A.C.P., and the Communists into doing something that so many people thought was bad.

But as I pedaled my bike away from the school that day, germs of doubt and questions crept into my mind. An image of Morgan staring at Ruby and the Cheerleaders in tight-lipped outrage lingered in my head. I tried to decipher his expression at that moment. His face seemed to communicate hurt, disbelief, confusion, and defiance, all at the same time. Why did he just stand there and watch? Why did he go nose-to-nose with Royce and Clem? Was he really a Communist spy? Was he a Jew? I'd never known a Communist or a Jew. Why did Communists and Jews want to manipulate the Negroes in the first place?

I pedaled by Rooms on Desire and did not see Morgan's car parked anywhere nearby. It was just before nine o'clock. Charlotte would arrive at nine thirty and start on the laundry. My only official duties at that hour were to be available for new arrivals and stay on call for Mr. Landroux. I knew Charlotte could cover me at least until noon, when she'd need help with lunch.

I didn't want to go back to the house. I needed time to think. So I steered past Rooms on Desire and pedaled my bike to the canal, letting all the random bits of information I had about Morgan stew in my head. Even though it was still early in the morning, a heavy humidity hung over the city. I could smell the earthy odor of the mud and waste rising from the canal, comfortingly familiar. I followed several pieces of garbage floating on top of the oily water, a ragged piece of *The Times-Picayune*, a blue five-gallon jug, a single white baby shoe. The shoe looked surprisingly new, and I wondered how it got there and hoped there wasn't a baby floating around somewhere in the water too. Jez claimed she saw a human hand sailing down the canal once, and I didn't doubt her. They had pulled more than a few bodies out of that water over the years.

I tried to unravel the mystery of Morgan in my head, but I kept coming up with more questions and no answers. So I headed toward the only other place that I suspected I might find him.

CHAPTER 17

I must confess that I felt a small rush of pride when I discovered Morgan's Bel Air parked across the street from Friendly Market on St. Claude. I really would make a good spy, I thought. Just as before, Morgan sat behind the wheel of his car smoking a cigarette and staring through the window of the store. I parked my bike and found a good observation post behind a milk truck.

I didn't see Morgan's brother, Michael, inside the store. A teenage boy with curly red hair stood behind the cash register reading a Green Lantern comic book. Again I made detailed notations in my Spy Log.

9:10 A.M.—Red-haired kid finishes Green Lantern comic and begins reading a Justice League of America comic.

9:22 A.M.—MM lights last cigarette and crumples pack.

9:27 A.M. —Short man buys shoe polish.

9:40 A.M.—Lady with red hair enters carrying a bag filled with rolled coins. She kisses the red-haired kid and gives him the coins, which he stores in the cash register. Lady exits.

9:42 A.M.—Red-haired lady appears in window of apartment on second floor above market. Must be family home.

9:50 A.M.—MM's brother, Michael, enters from back of store. Brother talks to red-haired boy. Red-haired boy exits. Brother puts on white apron and takes inventory with clipboard along aisle filled with canned vegetables.

Morgan watched his brother taking inventory for a few minutes. Finally he stepped out of the car.

He waited for some traffic to pass before crossing St. Claude, heading straight for the front entrance of the grocery. I needed to hear what they said to each other—watching them through a window simply would not do. I quickly rode my bike across the street and through the alley between the Chinese laundry and Friendly Market. I leaned my bike against a Dumpster and carefully approached the back door of the store. I moved close and ever so slowly opened the screen door, which squeaked and groaned like a tiny siren, wailing, "Look back here!" "Here I am!" and "There's a snoop in the store!" But once I slipped inside and gently let the door rest against its frame, I knew they hadn't heard me. I could hear their voices from somewhere in the front of the store. I didn't want to risk being seen, so I crouched behind a stack of cases of Dr Pepper at the end of an aisle, cocked an ear, and listened.

"When did you get into town?" Morgan's brother was asking.

"Yesterday," Morgan replied. "Morning."

"Where are you staying?"

"Little inn on Desire and North Galvez."

"Big green house?"

"Yeah."

"I've passed it before."

They fell into an uncomfortable beat of silence.

"The place looks good," Morgan said.

"Hasn't changed much."

"How're Edie and the kids?" Morgan asked.

"Fine."

"How're you?"

"Can't complain."

"You going to give me anything besides short answers?"

"I wasn't expecting to see you, Morgan."

"I was going to call first, but . . ." His voice trailed off.

"But?"

"But I wasn't sure what I would say on the phone," Morgan said.

"Do you have something to say now?"

"I wanted to see you, Michael."

"Not much has changed, has it?"

"I don't know," Morgan replied. "Things have changed for me."

"Well, you always liked change."

"I suppose I did."

Another awkward pause.

The way this conversation was going, it was difficult to imagine these two sitting in the same room for very long, never mind ever playing games together.

Morgan continued.

"I went by William Frantz this morning."

"Yeah?"

"Yeah. Pretty big mess, isn't it?"

"You could say that."

"She's a brave little girl."

"Who?"

"The little Negro girl."

"Yeah, right," Michael said.

"What's that supposed to mean?"

"Oh, come on, Morgan."

"What?"

"She's a puppet."

"That's pretty harsh."

"You really think she's got any idea what's going on?"

"I don't know. But that doesn't mean she's not brave to stand up to that mob every day."

"That mob has got a rooted interest in what goes on at that school."

"Oh God, Michael."

"It's easy for outsiders to come in and tell people what to do if they don't have to live with it."

"Outsiders?"

"You've been away a long time, Morgan."

"Don't tell me you agree . . . ?"

"Well, I don't disagree."

"How is this different from the Nazis, Michael?"

"Oh, please."

"No, really."

"It's very different."

"How?"

"You're being melodramatic."

"Am I?"

"No one is rounding up and killing Negroes, Morgan."

"Some people are."

"There's nothing wrong with separate schools."

"What about sending Jews to separate schools? That's how it started in Germany."

"This isn't Germany."

"Not yet."

"Give it a rest, Morgan."

"No. How is it different?"

"I don't want to hear one of your political speeches."

"Negroes are fighting for their rights as men just like the Jews did—"

"There's a big difference between Jews and Negroes, and you know it."

"No, I don't. Explain it."

"Is that why you came down here? To teach us backward yokels a lesson in morality?"

Morgan let the question settle for a moment before responding.

"No," he finally replied.

"Then why are you here?"

"I'm just here to see you."

"Why?"

"We're still family," Morgan said.

"Family." Michael repeated the word as if he didn't comprehend its meaning or use in the sentence.

"Yes. Family."

"So what does that mean exactly?"

"It means enough time has passed," Morgan said.

"Passed for what?"

"Well, for one thing, for me to forgive you."

"Forgive me?" Michael gasped.

"Yes."

"For what?"

"You know what," Morgan said.

"No. I honestly don't."

"Oh, come on, Michael, can we stop playing games?"

"I'm not playing a game. I can't for the life of me think of what *you'd* need to forgive *me* for."

Morgan exhaled and then replied. "How about for giving the committee my name?"

"I answered the questions they asked me," Michael responded, too quickly.

"Maybe you didn't have to give such complete answers."

"I didn't tell them anything they didn't already know."

"But you were happy to confirm things."

"Look, I wasn't happy about anything. I didn't have a choice."

"We all make choices, Michael."

"I wasn't gonna jeopardize my family just because you dragged me to a couple of meetings when we were barely out of high school. They had my name. I've got a life here. I could've lost everything. And I never joined anything."

"But you had no problem fingering your own brother."

"You were a Communist. Hell, you probably still are."

"So?"

"So, there's a war on."

"There wasn't then," Morgan replied. "Do you realize that if Joe McCarthy had been around in thirty-nine, I could've been blacklisted? Hell, I could've been thrown in jail."

"Those were bad times, Morgan."

"So it's okay to throw away the Bill of Rights during bad times?"

"Will you get off the goddamn soapbox already?"

"I'm not on a soapbox," Morgan said. "A lot of good people got hurt."

"And that's my fault?"

"If enough people had stood up—"

"Stood up for what? Stalin?"

"What I'm talking about has nothing to do with Stalin."

"Oh no?"

"Everyone should have the right to express their own political—"

"Oh, will you knock it off with the rhetoric? It's enough, Morgan. We've all had enough. Mama and Papa had enough. And now I've had enough. Okay?

"Don't bring them into this."

"Why not?"

"You don't speak for Mama and Papa."

"And you do?"

"I never claimed to."

"Got that right."

"What's that supposed mean?"

"Don't go there, Morgan."

"No. Say it."

"You pissed on everything they gave you."

"Bullshit."

"You don't think so?"

"You have no idea what they—"

"No. You're the one who's got no idea."

"You're crossing a line, Michael."

"What line?"

"You're crossing a line!"

"What the hell line are you talking about? Crossing lines? You're the one who came waltzing in here with all this bullshit about forgiving me for something you brought on yourself."

"That's enough."

"Do you really think Papa was proud of his Communist son?"

"Enough . . ."

"Poor old fool came over from the old country to give us better than he had—"

"I said that's enough!" Morgan snapped.

"They believed in this country. And so do I."

Then Michael added, half under his breath but loud enough for me to hear, "Maybe they *should've* thrown you in jail."

A long beat of silence followed. I heard both men breathing. Finally Morgan spoke.

"God, Michael, do you really hate me that much?"

Michael exhaled. "I don't know what I feel."

"We're still brothers," Morgan said.

"Why this sudden interest in reconnecting with family? Are you going to try to get us to join a protest outside of William Frantz?"

"No."

"Then what are you doing down here, Morgan?"

"I don't know."

"You're about thirty years too late to help out around the store."

I heard Morgan move toward the front door. "I guess you're right," he said. "Sorry I bothered."

I yearned for Michael to call out for him to stop, but he didn't. Did Michael know that Morgan's son had died in Korea? And did he know that Morgan and his wife had split? Why didn't Morgan say that he looked up to Michael when they were kids? And that he missed having an older brother? I couldn't understand why someone as articulate as Morgan could be so tongue-tied when it came to his own brother. Was he really going to walk away? After twenty years of silence, how could he let it end like that? I heard the front door slam open and shut, and I knew Morgan was gone. I slowly peered around the corner and caught a glimpse of Michael leaning over with one hand on the counter and the other pinching the bridge of his nose. He seemed deflated.

I didn't want to risk losing Morgan, so I turned to rush out the back door and ran straight into the red-haired kid, who was walking in carrying a big box of toilet paper rolls. I knocked the box to the floor and fell over.

"Hey!" the boy said.

Toilet paper rolls spilled out of the box. I tripped over them as I scrambled to my feet and ran out the back door.

CHAPTER 18

By the time I got back to St. Claude, Morgan's Bel Air was already gone. My legs ached from all the heavy pedaling I'd done that morning trying to keep up with him, so I don't know if I could've followed very far even if he had been within eyeshot. The sun beat down, and I reckoned it must've been around ten thirty by the time I started to walk my bike back home.

When I arrived, Morgan's car was not parked out front. Upon entering the kitchen, I found Charlotte hunched over the tub sink in the corner that we used for laundry, scrubbing a set of sheets.

She glared at me over her shoulder.

"Mr. Landroux had himself an accident."

"Oh," I said.

"Seems someone forgot to replace his bedpan this morning, and no one was around to bring him a new one when he rang his bell."

"Sorry."

"Sorry ain't cleaning these sheets."

"I'll do it," I said.

"That's right." She nodded. "You will."

She stepped away and washed her hands in the regular kitchen sink while I took over washing the sheets.

"Should I even ask where you were?" she said as she carefully dried her hands with a small blue-striped dish towel.

"I was just out . . . riding my bike . . . and I lost track of the time."

"I've told you before, Louise: I'd rather you not answer a question than lie straight to my face. Lying straight to someone's face is hurtful, particularly when it is someone you have a kinship with. Not answering a question is within your right of privacy, even with someone you have a kinship with. It's called taking the Fifth. You sure there's nothing you want to tell me?"

I did want to talk to her about everything, but I wasn't quite sure what to say. There were so many thoughts swirling around my head that I couldn't sort out. Should I tell her about Morgan being a Communist? Or my deep and true feelings for him? Or what happened at William Frantz this morning? I didn't really know where to begin. Not to mention the fact that so much of what I was thinking was brought about because of my snooping and spying, which did not reflect well on my character.

"I'll be taking the Fifth," I finally replied.

"I thought so," Charlotte said. "I don't know what's gotten into everybody, but your mother's got herself in a nasty mood today."

"Yeah?"

"She was stomping around, grousing about this and that before she went to the beauty shop."

"Do you know why she was upset?"

"Why?" Charlotte replied, incredulous. "Since when does that woman need a special reason to be in a bad mood? She just came back this morning all agitated. I'd try to keep my distance for a while if I were you."

She grabbed her purse from the counter and headed for the back door. "I'm going to get groceries. There's sliced ham in the icebox for lunch, and I left the jug of iced tea to brew out in the backyard."

She left, and I continued to scrub the sheets. As soon as she was gone, I regretted not opening up to her while I'd had the chance. Charlotte had a level head about most matters. I realized that part of my resistance to sharing with Charlotte had to do with Ruby Bridges and the desegregation issue. Of course I had always been fully aware that Charlotte was a Negro and that my mother and I were white. Yet racial politics had never played into our discussions. We had a primal connection that thrived within the confines of the house. When she wasn't being my guardian or teacher, she was my ally in labor. Yet some internal defense mechanism warned me that Charlotte might have opinions on integration that threatened the boundaries of our world.

CHAPTER 19

A knock at the front door interrupted my washing. I heard the familiar hard-edged voice of Ada Munson calling as she let herself in.

"Hello," she hollered. "Pauline, you 'round?"

I went out front and found Ada standing at the base of the stairs, looking up, a half-smoked cigarette hanging from her lips. Something about her always reminded me of a fire hydrant. She was a stout woman, with dirty reddish-brown hair that she wore in short, tight curls. She had cat's-eye tortoiseshell glasses on a chain, which magnified her squinty little eyes. One of the things that always drove me nuts about Ada was that she let her cigarettes burn down without ever flicking the ashes off, like she was too lazy to do it. Under the burden of their own weight the ashes would eventually fall off onto the front of her clothes or the floor. To me this was pure insanity. It was like she didn't care if she got her clothes dirty or lit herself on fire.

"Where y'at, girl?" she said when she saw me approach.

"Fine," I replied.

"Your mama home?" she asked.

"I haven't seen her," I said.

"She at da beauty shop?"

"Don't know. I think. Maybe."

"Got anyone staying with you?"

The question caught me off guard. I instinctively did not want to answer her, but there was no way to completely avoid the question without sounding suspicious.

"Yeah," I replied.

"Who?"

"A man," I said.

"Do you know da man's name?"

"No," I lied.

"Is he from New York?"

"I don't know."

"What kind of car is he driving?"

"I didn't see him drive up."

"Well, can you tell me what he looks like?"

"He's just a regular man. Not too young. Not too old."

"Oh, come on, Louise. You can do better den dat."

"He didn't take a meal with us," I lied, "so I didn't really see him much."

"Did your mama see him much?" she asked with a smirk.

"Huh?"

"Never mind," she said. "You're not a very useful snitch today, are you?"

I didn't respond.

"Be an angel and tell your mama dat she needs to give me a jingle."

Just then my mother walked in the front door. Her hair seemed to be styled her usual way. I'm not even sure she went to the beauty shop. She looked distracted and upset. I caught a flash of distress as it crossed her face when she saw Ada standing with me in the entry hall.

"Well, speak of da devil," Ada said with a grin. "Where y'at, Pauline?"

"Ada," my mother said in greeting as she hung up her light jacket on a coatrack we kept by the door. "This is a surprise."

"Just thought I'd come by and say hello, see how da business is going, Pauline."

"Same as ever. I'm not making the Hiltons nervous."

"I'm a little parched, dear," Ada said to me. "Could I trouble you for something cool?"

"Iced tea's still brewing out back," I said.

"Water'll be just fine," she offered.

The three of us moved to the kitchen. I retrieved two glasses and poured water for Ada and my mother.

"I heard tell you've got an interesting guest staying with you."

"Oh?"

"Da gentleman from New York."

My mother was turned away from Ada, but I could see the look of unease on her face. I could tell that like me, she instinctively did not want to answer any questions about Morgan.

"Nitty said he sounds like a real gentleman," Ada continued.

"I don't know."

"Oh, I think you know," Ada replied.

"Is there something you're trying to get at, Ada?"

"You don't have to be embarrassed, Pauline. You ain't da first girl to be duped by a Jew."

My mother turned to face Ada.

"Who said he's a Jew?"

"Oh, come on, Pauline. Now, I ain't no Miss Marple," Ada continued, "but I suspect dat your gentleman guest was da one who got in da scuffle with Royce and Clem dis morning. Derc were New York plates on his car."

"I didn't see the scuffle," my mother lied. "So I couldn't tell you."

"Well den, I'm telling you. Be careful."

Ada Munson drank down her water in a big long gulp. A small trickle ran down the side of her mouth, and she wiped it away with the back of her hand. She clapped the glass down on the counter.

"Just make sure he's gone double-quick. For his sake more dan yours."

My mother just stared at her for a long moment.

"You understand me, Pauline?"

My mother said, "Thanks for stopping by, Ada."

"Always a pleasure, Pauline. And thanks for da water."

Ada Munson let herself out, leaving my mother

and me alone in the kitchen. My mother stared out the back window for a long time, lost in thought. Her eyes seemed to be focused on nothing, just staring at a meaningless point on the back fence that bordered our house.

At that moment I felt close to my mother for the first time in a long time, like we were somehow bonded by our conflicted feelings for Morgan. I desperately wanted to know what she was thinking.

I watched her in silence for a few moments, then reached out a hand to her to see if I could offer some comfort or at least companionship. Maybe I would talk to her or she would talk to me, woman-to-woman. Whatever happened, I was ready. Gently I touched her back.

"Mama?" I felt off-balance, even slightly sick, but in some strange way quite grown-up.

"I've got a headache, Louise," she said, not turning around.

"But Mama, I—"

"Louise. Please. My head is throbbing. I need a moment's peace."

A lump rushed into my throat and shortened my breath. I turned and ran upstairs to my room and shut the door.

CHAPTER 20

Later that morning low gray clouds moved in over the city, but they just sort of hung there in the sky like a warning. The rest of the day I waited impatiently for Morgan to return, busying myself with little chores and activities around the house. My mother seemed to be waiting too, but she passed the time in a different way. Most days she mixed her lime juleps at one o'clock and then spent the rest of the afternoon listening to the radio. On this day she mixed herself a batch just before noon. She sat herself on the love seat rocker in the backyard. Yet she didn't listen to the radio.

She didn't fall asleep. She didn't even really rock in the love seat. She just waited and drank, drank and waited.

Charlotte returned from shopping just past noon and pushed her granny cart filled with groceries toward the back door. "Afternoon, Miss Pauline," she said to my mother as she passed. My mother didn't even look her way. She just stared off into space. Charlotte frowned. "I'm doing fine. Thank you for asking," Charlotte continued sarcastically as she struggled to pull the granny cart up the back steps. "It's okay. I got the door. Don't bother to get up."

I saw Charlotte from the kitchen and helped her to pull the cart inside.

"She's really in the bag today." She gestured to my mother outside. I nodded.

"Something happening with her? She doesn't usually take to drinking this early."

"I don't know," I said.

"Well, you better have some Bromo Seltzer ready tonight. She's gonna need it."

Charlotte and I unloaded the groceries and then spent the rest of the afternoon splitting chores and staying out of each other's way. I brought Mr. Landroux a sliced-ham-and-pickle po'boy and freshened his bed and then retreated to my room. I struggled to focus on *Jane Eyre* but couldn't keep my eyes on the page. I reread all my recent Spy Log entries, trying to gain some new insights into Morgan and the events of the past couple of days. I wound up spending most of the time watching and listening for a sign of Morgan's return.

My mother finished the pitcher of lime juleps around one o'clock. With some effort she hoisted herself out of the love seat rocker and walked into the kitchen, where she mixed another batch. Then she went right back to her routine, waiting and drinking, drinking and waiting. Finally, after consuming nearly two pints of cheap bourbon, six limes, and a handful of mint leaves, she passed out. She didn't look peaceful. Her face was pinched in a troubled expression, like she was squinting, trying to read some fine print on the back of her eyelids.

Late in the afternoon I helped Charlotte cook up a batch of her famous fiery rice and cheese. Charlotte believed this dish served as a natural hangover remedy, so she made it quite frequently. "The rice helps settle an angry stomach," she explained, "and the cayenne pepper purifies polluted blood." Charlotte's famous fiery rice and cheese recipe went something like this.

Cook two cups white rice and add the following:

2 tablespoons cayenne pepper

1 teaspoon black pepper

1 tablespoon salt

¾ pound of cheddar cheese (grated)

4 strips of crispy bacon (crumbled)

½ cup of green peas

¼ cup of milk

1 egg

Mix everything together in a cast-iron pot. Sprinkle the top with more bread crumbs,

cayenne pepper, and grated cheese.
Bake for 20 minutes.

Charlotte increased or decreased the level of
spice in the recipe depending on my mother's condition. That day she added an extra heaping teaspoon
of cayenne. Charlotte typically hummed and sang
gospel tunes as we worked. Sometimes I'd sing
along. My mother and I never took much religion,
so the words to the songs never really sank in very
deep or had much meaning for me. They were just
melodies and words that provided a way to pass the
time. But on this day everything seemed to take on
heightened significance, including the final verse of
"Get on Board, Little Children." She must've sung
that song a thousand times, but I never really took
notice of what the words about the gospel train
might imply about her view of the world.

> *The fare is cheap and all can go;*
> *The rich and poor are there.*
> *No second class aboard this train;*

No difference in the fare.
So get on board, little children;
Get on board, little children.
Get on board, little children;
There's room for many a-more.

By the time we put the pot in the oven to cook, it was already five fifteen and Morgan had not yet returned. The sky darkened as the sun went down behind the heavy clouds. My mother still slept out back as Charlotte packed herself up to leave. Charlotte turned to look at me. I could tell by her expression that she knew something was brewing with me and my mother.

"What?" I said.

"You wanna tell me what?" she replied.

We stood staring at each other until there was a knock at the front door. The sound made me jump.

"Evening," Morgan called. "Anyone home?"

I looked down at myself in a panic. I wore a food-smudged apron and my face and hands were a mess. I couldn't let him see me like this. I glanced at

Charlotte, silently pleading. She understood. She put down her bag and took off her coat.

"Clean yourself up. I'll do the greeting. But then I've gotta get home. You hear?"

CHAPTER 21

I heard Charlotte greet Morgan as I whipped off the apron and tried to scrub myself down as best I could. One question throbbed in my head: Should I attempt to wake my mother? If she was ever going to make it out to Commander's Palace, she would need to sober up fast. I wasn't sure if it was better to let her sleep it off for a few more minutes or wake her up to give her longer to sober up. Another more sinister part of me wanted her to just sleep the night away so I could have him all to myself. I'd just tell him she was called away on a family emergency out of town. Maybe he would take me to Commander's Palace in her place.

Charlotte returned to the kitchen.

"Your guest would like some lemonade," she said. "He's in the Music Hall."

"Thanks," I said.

"Now I'm going home."

She looked out the window at my mother and shook her head.

"Don't let her stay out there too long or she'll likely catch something."

"I won't," I said.

Charlotte put her coat back on and moved to the back door.

"You sure you're all right, Louise?"

She waited for an answer this time.

"Come on, girl," she said. "I ain't got all night."

She stared at me another moment until her big cat eyes wore me down.

"I like him."

"Uh-huh," she grunted in a noncommittal way.

"There's nothing wrong with me just liking someone."

"No. But I get the sense there's more going on than you just liking this man."

I didn't respond.

"Louise, sometimes the best thing about being a child is that you don't have to involve yourself in grown-up things. You understand? You've got plenty of time to get mixed up in all sorts of grown-up trouble later."

"I'm not getting in any trouble."

"Just try not to, all right?"

I didn't respond. She shook her head and said, "Don't forget to take the pot out of the oven." She walked out the back door and shook her head again as she passed my mother on the way back around to the front of the house.

When I brought him the lemonade, Morgan was sitting in the wing chair by the front window, reading the sports section of *The Times-Picayune*.

"Thank you, Miss Louise."

"Sure," I said, handing him the glass.

He folded the paper and clapped it on the end table beside him.

"The Knicks will be lucky to win five games this year. You follow basketball?"

"Can't say that I do," I replied.

"Good thing you're not a Knicks fan. They're just horrible this season. Syracuse beat 'em by sixty-one points a few weeks ago."

"Is that bad?" I asked.

"Worst loss in the team's history."

"You're a big sports fan, huh?"

"Everything except hockey. It's not a good sport for writers. The puck moves too fast. Never enough time to rhapsodize about what you're seeing. All the best sportswriting is about baseball, because it's got so many natural pauses, it gives you time to reflect."

"You write about sports?" I asked, thinking he might confess his affiliation with the Communist newspaper.

"Every now and then I write for a small paper back in New York. I don't make a living at it."

Again I found myself struggling for something clever to say. All I could come up with was "Did you have a nice day?"

"Not really," he said.

"I'm sorry."

"Don't be. It's not your fault."

"Did you see your family?"

I dangled the question out there, hoping he would reveal himself. A rush of adrenaline hit me as I asked the question, as if I were completing the most illicit dare. It felt dangerous even to ask, given what I knew about what had happened, like I was risking something for both of us.

He gave me a sad smile.

"Yeah. My brother. But things didn't turn out quite the way I'd hoped."

"How do you mean?"

"Well, Michael and I don't really get along, and we haven't for a long, long time."

"Why not?" I asked, emboldened by his honesty.

"It's complicated. I guess we both hurt each other over the years. And then we had a big fight and never made up. I guess that when you have a falling-out with someone, like we did, you can't wait too long to try to make up or it just gets to be too late. It feels like too much time has passed to get back to anywhere near where we used to be."

"Why would it be too late?"

"You ask tough questions."

"I'm sorry."

"No. It's all right." He paused a moment to think. "I suppose we both just can't shift off the feelings that have set in over the years. You know, one of the things they tell you when you get married is 'Never go to bed angry at each other,' because if you do, your angry feelings harden overnight and become that much tougher to shake off the next morning. Well, my brother and I have been going to bed angry at each other for twenty years."

"Are you going to try to see him again?"

"Tell you the truth, I don't know quite yet. We make each other so mad, neither of us is thinking straight. I'm trying to settle my mind before I make any decisions about what to do."

"Well, it seems to me like if you came down all this way just to see him, it's probably worth another try. You know, just to see. Because maybe he's thinking about you right now. And feeling bad about things."

"You may be right about that."

"I bet I am. Really. You shouldn't give up."

"Did you ever think about becoming a psychiatrist?"

"I'm not quite sure I know what that is."

He laughed.

"It's a doctor who helps people work through their problems. You seem to have a knack for it."

"Thank you . . . I guess."

He laughed again.

"Well, why don't you tell me how your day was?"

"It wasn't bad, I guess." I felt a deep pang of

guilt that I had spent the most interesting part of my day searching his room and eavesdropping on his private conversations.

"How was school?" he asked.

"I don't go to school."

"No?"

"Well, not right now. There's a boycott on. No one really goes."

"Do you know why there's a boycott?"

"Integration," I said.

"What about integration?" he asked.

"Folks around here are against it. And the federal government wants it."

"Are you against it?"

No one had ever asked me this question before.

"I don't know," I said.

"Do you think it'd be wrong to go to school with Negro kids?"

"I don't know that it would make any difference. We don't have the best teachers at my school."

He chuckled.

"Do you ever play with Negro kids?"

"No."

"Why not?"

"I don't really play with many kids at all," I confessed.

"That's a shame," he said. "Why is that?"

"I don't know. I guess I'm not that interested in the stuff that most kids are interested in around here."

"You're just more mature than they are."

"You think so?"

"I know it. When I grew up here, I felt the same way," he said. "I was always good at schoolwork and bad at sports. And for a boy that's a terrible combination. Guess that's why I'm such a big sports fan. I love watching people who are good at something I'm not. But let me tell you, there's a world of people out there, Louise. All sorts of people who are more like you than you can imagine. You're gonna grow up and find a whole bunch of friends who like to read and do all the things you like to do and then some. Never ever be ashamed of being smart, Louise. That brain of yours will take you places and show you things. You trust me on that."

At that moment I had never felt such a powerful connection to another human being. I was ready to declare myself a sports fanatic, a Communist, or anything else to solidify my allegiance to Morgan. Perhaps we could move to the Soviet Union and work on some farming commune together.

"Hold on just a sec. I want to give you something," he said, suddenly rising.

He ran back outside to his car, which was parked in front of the house. He opened the trunk and rummaged around for a minute before he found what he was looking for—a book. He tucked it under his arm and closed the trunk. When he returned, he handed me a hardbound copy of John Steinbeck's novel *The Grapes of Wrath*.

"Have you read it?" he asked.

"No," I replied.

"It's probably his best. Although I wouldn't tell him that. It's also a long one, so stick with it to the end."

"I will."

"Look inside," he said.

The book felt heavy and important.

"Go on, open it," he encouraged.

I opened the book and saw the following message written in black ink on the flyleaf.

Dear Morg,

You're a lousy drinker, but a damn good friend.

Thanks for putting up with all of my BS.

All the best,

John Steinbeck

I gently ran my index finger across the page, awed by the fact that Steinbeck's hand had touched it.

"You sure you want me to have this?" I asked.

"Yep."

"But he gave it to you."

"I'm sure he wouldn't mind."

"Really?"

"Really." He nodded.

"I don't know how to thank you for something like this."

"You can thank me by reading and enjoying it."

"I will. I promise."

He checked his watch. "And now I think I'd better find your mother."

"My mother . . ."

"We've got dinner reservations at six thirty. I hear the folks at Commander's Palace can get awfully fussy if you're late."

CHAPTER 22

When I walked back into the kitchen, a small trail of smoke leaked out the top of the oven. It wasn't the first time I'd let my mind wander and burned the supper. I rushed over, grabbed two oven mitts, took out the pot of fiery rice and cheese, and laid it on the stove. The bread crumbs on the top were burned, but the rest was salvageable. Looking out the window, I saw my mother slumped over in the love seat rocker. She typically slept in a fairly dignified, upright position, like a lady of leisure taking an afternoon nap. Now she looked more like a drunk who had passed out.

She was in no condition to trot off to Commander's Palace or anywhere else, for that matter.

I ran out the back door and tried to shake her awake.

"Mama!" I hissed at her. "Mama—*wake up*!"

But she wouldn't stir. I felt her hot breath on me as I pushed my body against her shoulder in an attempt to hoist her back to a normal sitting position. Unfortunately, her body tilted over in the other direction until she tipped over and hung off the side of the rocker like the old Howdy Doody puppet I kept on top of my dresser. I ran around and pushed her back the other way, managing to balance her in something resembling a sitting position.

"Mama . . . please wake up!" I pleaded.

I ran back inside and retrieved a glass of ice water, reasoning that if I could get her to take a drink, it might revive her. I wasn't sure how I would get the water down her throat. So first I fished a piece of ice out of the glass and ran it across her forehead. She jerked and twisted her neck and made a small grunt in reaction to the cold, but her eyes remained closed. I raised the glass to her lips and tilted her head back.

"Here, Mama. Drink."

I attempted to slowly pour some water into her mouth. As soon as the water hit her throat, she coughed so violently that her right arm jerked in a spasm, knocking the glass from my hand. It shattered on the ground beneath my feet. Her coughing escalated until she started gagging. Her throat emitted a horrible, bubbled wheeze. Then it happened— she vomited all over the place, covering herself in yellow bile flecked with half-chewed pieces of mint leaves.

I grabbed her as she heaved again, hoping to direct the vomit onto the ground, but I wound up covered myself, all down the front of my clothes. This was not the first time I'd seen my mother sick from drinking, but it was the first time I had been caught in the line of fire. The violence of the vomiting shook her awake a little. She tried to steady herself on the love seat. I'm sure the motion of the rocker wasn't helping right then. She heaved and vomited a third time and was at least able to direct it away from herself and me and into the flower bed beside the rocker. When she was finished, she gasped for breath.

"Louise . . . goddamn . . ." she rasped.

She heaved again, but nothing came up this time, just a gurgling sound and then a dry rasping gasp. Her face was as red as a firecracker, and her eyes looked like they might pop out of her head.

"Water . . ." she said.

I ran back inside to get another glass, and I discovered Morgan standing in the kitchen. I froze when I saw him. He looked me up and down.

"Is everything all right?" he asked.

Here I was, covered in my mother's vomit, in the midst of trying to revive her so she could go on a date with him—a Communist who might be a full-blown spy or a least an agitator. Nothing was all right.

"No," I replied, running past him.

"My God, what happened?"

I ignored the question and ran back outside

with the glass of water. Morgan followed. Again I attempted to feed my mother a drink of water. Morgan rushed over and helped prop her up. He steadied her while I poured a small amount of water into her mouth. She gagged a bit but was able to swallow it. She took another sip and her breathing calmed. Her eyes finally began to focus. She recoiled when she saw that Morgan was holding her.

"Get your damn hands off me!" She twisted away from him and even managed to stand up.

"Hey, it's okay," he said.

"No! It's not okay!" my mother snapped back.

"Just relax," he said, genuinely surprised.

"Mama, he was only helping."

"Shut up, Louise!"

"But Mama . . ."

"I said shut up. And get upstairs!"

"Pauline," Morgan tried to reason, "aren't you being a little—"

"Get upstairs, Louise! Now!"

Overwhelmed by shame, hurt, and my pure helplessness in the situation, I burst out crying. I couldn't speak. Like my mother's jagged demeanor, my tears came out raw and ugly.

"You heard me," she rasped. "Git!"

I blubbered for another moment and ran inside the house and up to my room.

CHAPTER 23

When I got to my room, I threw myself on my bed, sobbing in big hearty gusts. I could hear their voices carrying up from the backyard. I remember thinking that for the first time in my life, I didn't want to spy. I didn't want to hear anything that my mother might say, because I knew it wasn't going to be pretty. But I couldn't move; something compelled me to listen, like when people rush over to see a house burn down or watch bloody victims pulled from a train wreck.

"Are you a Jew?" my mother said, slurring.

"Excuse me?"

"I don't want to be deceived anymore."

"I haven't deceived you."

"Are you a Jew?"

"I don't practice any religion."

"I haven't choked down a Communion wafer in ten years, but that don't mean I'm not half Catholic."

"What difference does—?"

"ARE YOU A JEW?"

"I was born Jewish," he said. "Does that matter?"

"Does that matter?" my mother gasped. "Of course it matters."

"What's gotten into you?"

"What are you doing here?" she countered.

"I don't understand what you mean."

"What the hell are you doing here?"

"I needed a room."

"In New Orleans. What are you doing in New Orleans?"

"I came down to see my brother."

"You're lying!"

"I'm not lying."

"Then what were you doing at the school this morning?"

"Were you there?" he asked.

"Yes. I was there," she said. "And I saw you."

"Are you one of the Cheerleaders?"

"I've got nothing to hide."

"Neither do I."

"Then what were you doing at the school?"

"I wanted to see it with my own eyes. I didn't quite believe it."

"Believe what?"

"Everything," he said.

"You're one of the Northern Jews who're stirring up the niggers and making all this trouble."

"I wasn't making any trouble."

"You're some kind of organizer."

"That's not true."

"You're lying again."

"No, I'm not. But I'm certainly not against what's happening."

"So you just went over there to look around, like a tourist waltzing down Bourbon Street."

"I went over there to get a look at what real courage looks like. It's not every day you get to see that."

"Real courage."

"That little Negro girl has got more courage than anyone I've ever seen. And I felt like I needed to find a little courage to face my brother."

"You mean to tell me that's the only reason you were there?"

"Yes. Why were *you* there?"

"What do you mean, why was I there? This is my neighborhood. I belong there."

"No one belongs taunting an innocent child."

"*Innocent,*" my mother scoffed.

"She's only six years old."

"She's part of the whole conspiracy."

"What conspiracy?

"The niggers and the Jews trying to take control."

"Take control of what?"

"Everything."

"She just wants a better education. Doesn't evcryone deserve an education?"

"Nigger-loving propaganda."

"It's not propaganda."

"Why do you care so much about the niggers?"

"I try to care about everybody."

"Isn't that just dandy. You know what I think?"

"No."

"I think everybody should just mind themselves."

"What kind of harm would it do if that little girl went to school in the same building with your little girl?"

"I don't want to get into a political conversation."

"But it's not political to you, is it? It's personal, right?"

"Damn straight it's personal," she snapped back. "We oughta be able to decide what kind of school we want for our own children. The government's got no right coming in here and telling us how to live our lives."

"Don't you think Negro parents feel the same way?"

"I don't give a goddamn what the hell Negro parents think. Of course they want what we've got. White people build up everything, and then Negroes just come along and think they can take it and dirty it up. We've got a right to control our own neighborhood."

"It's their neighborhood too."

"It's not their neighborhood. White people built this city when most of them were swinging from trees in Africa. I know how they live. They drink like fish and breed like monkeys in the jungle. And they're violent like angry cats."

"You don't really believe what you're saying."

"Damn right I do. I've seen them up close. Human life just doesn't mean as much to the niggers. Most of them are barely human."

"You should be ashamed of yourself."

"I'm ashamed of nothing."

"Do you want your daughter growing up thinking like that?"

"Keep her out of this."

"You're responsible for raising that child. Lord knows what kind of hateful ideas you're putting in her head."

"Don't talk to me about responsibility!" My mother's voice cracked. The entire conversation she had been slurring and angry, but managed to keep her voice somewhat level. Now her voice became more and more strained, rising in pitch like a boiling tea kettle. "I've done right by that child," she continued. "No one's gonna tell me I haven't, goddamn it. I've done more right than any woman would've in my situation. I've given that girl a proper home. I've fed her. I've clothed her. I've raised her up from a baby. Changed diapers. Taught her to talk. Oh, and the money I've spent. New shoes! Haircuts! Clothes! Notebooks! Pencils! Lunch boxes! Glasses! Presents at Christmas! You name it. Goddamn it! I did it! Do you hear? I did it!"

"Isn't that what a mother's supposed to do for her daughter?" Morgan asked.

My mother's response shook me more than I ever thought a simple sentence of the English language could.

"I am not her mother."

Those five little words hit my brain like a bucket of freezing-cold water, sending a chill through my entire body. My mind raced back over my previous thirteen years, and snippets of memory rose up and hit me in the face, a thousand little moments that made me know instantly that what she said was absolutely true.

"What do you mean?" Morgan asked.

"I mean what I said," my mother responded, her voice softening but cracking under the weight of a small sob. "I'm not her mother."

"I don't understand."

She paused to catch her breath. The anger

drained from her voice like the confession had blown it out of her. "She's my sister's child."

"Your sister," he said.

"They ran off together, she and Duane, just a few months after we hit Baton Rouge. They were wild, both of them. Born wild. She came back a few months later all knocked up. He stayed in Kansas City or wherever he was and let her have the baby alone. Just a couple of days after she gave birth, she took off again and left the baby behind. Didn't even give her a name. I had to register the birth down at the city hall, and I just put myself down as her mother. I knew they wouldn't be back."

"How did you know?"

"They were junkies. Morphine. He got her started on the stuff, but then she took to it like a bird to flying. They moved around a lot. St. Louis, then Detroit, then Louisville. I think he left her in Cleveland. I heard from her once, maybe twice a year, usually scratching around for money. But of course I never had any. Then about five years ago I got a call from the Cleveland coroner's office. She overdosed. I think she had been selling herself to keep her habit going. I didn't claim the body. I don't even know where they buried her or if they even bothered to do it at all."

"And Louise doesn't know anything?" he asked quietly.

"What would be the point?" She sighed.

CHAPTER 24

So there it was. My mother was not a Cheerleader. My mother was a whore and a junkie. And now she was dead. And what did that make me? Did I inherit a heart that would allow me to abandon my own baby? I wasn't anyone's baby. I wasn't anyone's little girl. I was just a burden. I'd always felt like a stranger with my mother. Always. And now I knew why.

As shaken and upset as I was by my mother's revelation, the news of my true identity had actually made me stop crying. In the silence I noticed an unfamiliar noise coming from below. It took me a moment to fully comprehend that it was the sound of my mother crying. Over the years I'd seen my mother yell, scream, howl, and pout, but never really cry. In difficult situations she typically got angry but never weepy. The alien sound of her crying was surprisingly high-pitched and fragile, like the tears had opened up a crack inside her and let a little girl come out.

I willed myself to stand up and peek out of the corner of my window. When I looked into the backyard, I saw Morgan holding my mother in a tight embrace. Her shoulders rose and fell under the cadence of her sobs. They stood together for at least two minutes, with Morgan gently rubbing his hands against her upper back and shoulders. He softly whispered, "It's okay, it's okay," over and over until her crying subsided. Finally, she pulled away from him. The crying had made red bags well up under her eyes, and her mascara ran in gray lines down her cheeks. Her hair seemed to be hanging off to the left side of her head like a fallen cake. And her clothes were rumpled, creased, and splattered with her own bile. But the emotional outburst seemed to sober her up quick. Her voice returned to something resembling normal, and she suddenly snapped into tight focus.

"You've got to leave," she said.

"Why?"

"People know you're here."

"So?"

"It could be real trouble for both of us. I can't take any more trouble in my life than I've already got."

He stared at her.

"You're kidding, right?"

"No. This neighborhood's like an angry hornet's nest right now. You've really got to go tonight and lay low," she said.

"You mean it, don't you?"

"I'm sorry."

He nodded.

"There's an inn on St. Claude. The Merriweather. I'll call over—"

"Don't worry about it," he said. "I'll find a place."

Morgan moved to her, held her shoulders, and planted a kiss on her forehead. It was a tender, fatherly kiss, like he was trying to make her feel better about something. Then he turned and walked back into the house. My mother collapsed onto the love seat rocker, buried her face in her hands, and cried again.

I heard Morgan trudge upstairs and close the door to his room. That's when it started to rain. My mother sat in the downpour for a couple of minutes, letting it soak her completely. Finally she retreated inside and up to her room. When I heard the sound of her drawing a bath, I made my decision.

CHAPTER 25

It was probably only around seven thirty. The rain made it seem much later than it actually was, because most people had escaped indoors. The streets were empty and the thick clouds and fog blotted out any light from the sky or surrounding houses. The only light in the immediate vicinity was the yellow-gray haze thrown from the window of Morgan's room and the greenish glow from a small bulb that lit our sign advertising Rooms on Desire.

As I stood beside Morgan's Bel Air, staring at the sign, I believed it might be the last time I'd ever see my house. The rain soaked through my shoes and socks, and my toes were getting numb from the cold. I had thrown a few essential clothes, my Spy Logs, and Morgan's copy of *The Grapes of Wrath* into my small suitcase and run out the door while my mother's bathwater was still running. I didn't want to risk her hearing me leave. I'd forgotten an umbrella, but I had resolved never to go back inside the house again. I figured I could tolerate a few minutes of being wet for a new life.

The light went out in the second-story front bedroom, and a moment later Morgan walked out of our house carrying his suitcase, his briefcase, and an umbrella. He closed the front door and came walking toward me. I straightened up my posture in a small but pathetic attempt to present the most inviting picture possible, not really comprehending how much I must have resembled a scrawny, wet sheepdog with glasses. Due to the darkness, he didn't even see me until he reached the car. His face registered a small sad grin when he laid eyes on me, stringy hair matted to my head and glasses all fogged up. I picked up my suitcase.

"Take me with you," I said.

"Oh, Miss Louise."

"Please."

"You heard everything?"

I nodded. "There's no reason for me to stay."

He bent down next to me so his umbrella covered both our heads.

"Honey, I can't take you."

"Why?"

"Well, first of all, I'd be arrested for kidnaping."

"She wouldn't care."

"I think she would."

"She's not even my mother."

"Well, she may not have given birth to you, but—"

"She doesn't give a lick about me," I interrupted.

"I don't think that's true."

"You don't understand."

"No, I probably don't. But I think she needs you."

"Of course she needs me! I do all the work!"

"Look, she's your family. You've gotta hold on to

that. And like I said before, you just wait. Life is going to open up for you, Louise. Never think that your prospects are limited to the borders of the Ninth Ward. I never did."

"Please. Take me."

"Oh . . . Miss Louise. You know I can't."

So I broke down and started bawling. I must confess that at least a small part of the crying was a last-ditch play on his sympathies.

"I don't want you to leave."

He hugged me tightly.

"You can call or write me anytime," he said. "I'm a great correspondent. And I'm expecting you to let me know what you thought of *The Grapes of Wrath* when you're finished."

My eyes were downcast. A cross-country pen pal was not what I'd been hoping for.

He gently lifted my chin with his hand.

"I mean it, Miss Louise. You're a special girl. You haven't heard the last of me. I promise. Here's how to reach me."

He removed a business card from his wallet and

handed it to me. I wiped my eyes and slipped the card into my pocket.

"Now you'd better go dry off or you'll catch something."

He stood up and kissed me on the forehead in almost the exact spot where I'd seen him kiss my mother. Then he moved away, threw his bags in the trunk, and got behind the wheel. I held my ground. I wasn't going to make it easy for him. So I posed like the sad wet dog that I was and watched as he started the engine, gave me a final wave that seemed to be saying both "good-bye" and "sorry," and drove off toward St. Claude.

I'd always been a lonely kid. I always felt like I was an adult running around in a kid's body and like all the other kids knew it. I wasn't fooling them. Despite thirteen years of solid loneliness, I'd never felt as desperately alone as at that moment.

As I watched Morgan's taillights disappear into the fog on Desire, all the energy seemed to drain out of my body. I literally couldn't find the strength or motivation to move from the spot I was standing on.

My feet were completely soaked and stiff from the cold, as if they were frozen to the sidewalk. As the rain continued to pelt me, I thought I just might stand there and let myself catch pneumonia or die of exposure. I must have stood like that for at least twenty minutes, until the top of my head started to go numb from the cold and the rhythm of the rain.

I truly believe I might've stayed like that until I collapsed if it hadn't been for the small familiar sound that cut through to my chilled brain. At first I was in such a haze that I couldn't identify what the sound was, even though my body was already reacting to it. The noise was light and slightly musical. Some deeply ingrained Pavlovian response caused my feet to move back toward the house to answer the muffled tinkle of Mr. Landroux's bell coming from the third floor.

CHAPTER 26

I dropped my jacket and suitcase in my room before proceeding to the top floor. My mother's door was shut when I passed, but I knew she was in there because the light was on and I could here the faint buzz of her radio—Rosemary Clooney's pidgin Italian, "Botch-a-me, I' botcha-you and ev'rything goes crazy." She always ignored Mr. Landroux's bell when she knew I was around. My hair was still dripping wet when I entered his room. I remember for the first time in my life experiencing a small sense of relief at the sight of Mr. Landroux.

"I thought you'd forgotten about me, Four Eyes," he said. Thankfully, he didn't seem to be in the midst of one of his spells.

"Sorry. I was downstairs."

"Looks like you took a bath in your clothes."

"I had to go outside."

"Ever hear of a little thing called an umbrella?"

"I couldn't find one. You need something?"

"I've got an itch dat's been bothering me something fierce."

He leaned forward, gesturing to his lower back. Because he spent all day in bed, he was prone to developing bedsores. They often became extremely irritated, because he would incessantly scratch them. Sometimes he scratched so hard, he would break the skin and his dirty fingernails would cause them to become infected. We kept a bottle of rubbing alcohol and a glass jar filled with cotton balls on his dresser for when this happened. I wet a cotton ball with alcohol as he hiked up the back of his pajama shirt. Several small red sores the size of nickels ran across the bottom of his back, just above the elastic waistband of his pants. The skin was raised in the sores, in strange swirling patterns, but luckily he hadn't broken the skin. I gently dabbed at the sores with the alcohol. He let out small moans of pain and relief with each swipe. After I'd gone through several cotton balls, he lowered his shirt.

"Thanks, Four Eyes," he said. "I'll tip you at Christmas, okay?"

This was what Mr. Landroux would say whenever he truly wanted to show gratitude, and he was grateful. He needed me. I believe that he honestly thought he would, in fact, tip me at Christmas. And he always waited for me to acknowledge the offer.

"Okay," I said. "Christmas it is."

He gave me a small smile and laid his head back against his pillow.

CHAPTER 27

Despite his physical ailments, Mr. Landroux tended to sleep soundly through the night. Even under the best conditions I did not. As I lay in bed that night, the downpour tapered off to a slow drizzle. I heard the runoff in the gutter that ran down the side of the house beside my window decrease to a trickle. In contrast with the rain outside that was drying up, a newly secreted venom was coursing through my body like an out-of-control river about to burst a dam. Every few moments my body shuddered in an involuntary reaction to the poison. Several toxic hates fed the venom. I hated

my father for being a junkie, and for being completely absent. I hated my natural mother for having
me and abandoning me and being a junkie and for
dying. And I hated the lost opportunity to hate. And
I hated myself for being the child of such wretched
souls.

But most of all I hated my mother, or Aunt
Pauline, or whoever she was. Not for the way she
had raised me, not for making me work since as
far back as I could remember. Not for her being a
drunk or a racist. No, I hated her for driving away
the first person who had ever offered me a small
beacon of hope in my dreary little world. For the
briefest moment Morgan Miller had been my ideal
father, brother, teacher, friend, Edward Rochester,
and Prince Charming all rolled into one. And life
had seemed a little less bleak. But just as quickly
as he appeared, he was gone, and at her request.
And why had she driven him away? Because Ada
Munson and Nitty Babcock would talk? Because
he was a Jew? Because he believed that little black
kids should go to school with little white kids?

What did any of that really matter?

A sudden noise from outside made me snap to attention. A car or truck pulled to a stop in front of the house. At first my pulse quickened at the thought that Morgan had returned. But then I heard at least two doors open and shut and two sets of heavy footsteps walking toward the house. It must have been nine or ten o'clock, which was usually too late for new business. A moment later the front door crashed open, and I heard two bodies stumble inside.

"Pauline!" Royce bellowed. "Pauline, where da hell are you at? We want to have a party with one of your guests."

I heard Clem's strange throaty giggle. Even though he was a big man, Clem had an unusually high-pitched speaking voice, and he giggled like a dumb little kid who'd just got caught writing dirty words in a hymnbook. They both sounded like they had been drinking for quite a while.

"We brought some homemade beignets and jam," Royce continued.

"And little party hats," Clem added.

"Pauline!"

I heard my mother's door open.

"Will you quit shouting like that!" she yelled down at them, descending the stairs.

"Don't want to disturb your guest?" Royce asked.

"I don't have any guests right now," she said.

"Dat's not what we heard." Clem giggled again.

"We heard you've got someone special staying over," Royce added. "Real special."

"Well, whoever you're talking about is gone now," she said.

"Really?" Royce asked sarcastically.

"Really," my mother replied.

"Oh, what a shame," Royce said. "'Cause we're throwing a real nice party for him."

"It's BYOR," Clem said. "Bring Your Own Rope."

Clem and Royce laughed.

"Like I said, he's gone," she said.

"Gone?" Royce said.

"Yes. I made him leave," she replied.

"Why'd you go and do dat?" Royce asked. "You trying to spoil da party?"

She didn't answer.

"Where did he go?" Clem said.

"How am I supposed to know?" she replied.

"Well, I'm sure you showed him some of your usual Southern hospitality. People who get all intimate like that tend to share personal details."

"We didn't get intimate," she said.

"Not what I heard," Royce countered.

"Well, whatever y'all heard ain't true," she said.

"Nitty Babcock's pretty reliable when it comes to these things."

"Nitty Babcock doesn't know everything that goes on around here."

"Well, I've got a pretty good idea," Royce countered.

"Look, he's gone. And I don't have any idea where he is. Y'all can keep asking, but it isn't gonna make me know something I don't know."

"It don't matter none," Royce said. "We got his

car make and plates. Everyone knows what to look for. We'll find him."

"Well, I don't want to keep you," she said. "And if you don't mind, I need to get some shut-eye."

"Oh, we were hoping to get us a little motivation while we're here," Royce said.

"Yeah. We need someone to grease our wheels." Clem grunted and giggled.

"I'm not really feeling so well tonight," she said.

"What?" Royce gasped in mock surprise. "Did dat Jew wear you out, Pauline?"

"Really, nothing happened between me and him. And I just need to go to bed—"

"Oh, no you don't," Royce snapped. I heard a sharp slap, and my mother gasped in shocked pain.

"Royce, please—"

I heard them shuffling and furniture moving.

"Stop," she pleaded.

"Shut up!" Royce roared.

I heard clothes ripping.

"Oh yeah." Clem clucked.

I pressed my hands over my ears as hard as I

could, but I couldn't block out the noise from below. I knew that unlike the other times, she did not want to be part of what was happening down in the Music Hall tonight. My mind scrabbled with panic for my mother but also for Morgan. They had his car make and plates. They knew what to look for. "We'll find him," Royce had said with absolute certainty. Behind my closed eyes I saw images of burning crosses and Morgan's bloody body swinging from a tree like the black-and-white newspaper photographs of teenage Negro boys after a lynching.

Another loud crash from downstairs caused my eyes to snap open again. She was in real trouble. I had to do something, but I didn't know what. I rose out of my bed and opened my door. As I moved toward the stairs, the noise from below grew louder and more menacing.

I paused at the top of the stairs and looked into the darkness below. Then I took a deep breath and walked down. When I reached the bottom step, I softly called out, "Mama? Are you all right?" She did not reply.

I walked to the entrance to the Music Hall and called again, a little louder, "Mama?" I stopped in the doorway and stared into the room. She was lying across the couch, with Royce on top of her with his pants bunched down at his ankles. Clem stood over them, watching and waiting. As soon as I came into sight, Clem laughed.

"All right! Now we've got a party!"

Royce ignored me and kept grunting. My mother's head turned and her eyes met mine. Her face was pinched in pain and streaked with tears. She shouted, "Get out of here!"

I hesitated for just a moment. She screeched at me again.

"Get *out!*"

I turned and ran out the back door of the house. I pulled my bike out of the shed and fled down the street as fast as my feet could pedal.

CHAPTER 28

Charlotte Dupree lived with her elderly mother in a tiny square redbrick house in a Negro section of the ward just a few minutes' bike ride from Rooms on Desire. I had seen the interior of Charlotte's house only once before. It was back in the summer of 1958, when her father passed away after suffering a severe stroke at the lunch counter of a Negro po'boy shack called Ragin' Ray's. My mother and I did not attend the funeral. When I asked her why not, she simply said, "It wouldn't be proper." But later that day my mother sent me over to the house to deliver a small bouquet of flowers and a homemade pot of gumbo.

It was one of the rare instances I remember my mother preparing anything in the kitchen aside from her daily dose of lime juleps. I watched her cook in true astonishment, not so much because it was such a rarity, but because of the ease with which she threw everything together. She chopped the green onions and okra with the precision of an expert. And she didn't even use a measuring spoon to add in the spices. She just tossed them in like a pro who could measure amounts by how the ingredients felt in her hands. Hell, she didn't even consult a recipe book once. Sometime in her past my mother had been a cook, and a good one.

The death of Charlotte's father also provided one of the only times I remember my mother saying something that I thought to be truly insightful. After she finished preparing the gumbo, she gave me the pot to deliver.

"What do I say to her?" I asked.

"Just tell her that we're very sorry about the loss of her daddy."

"Is that it?" I asked. It didn't seem like enough.

"A full stomach is one of the only things that can truly lessen sorrow," she said. "That's why you see so many fat people around here."

When I delivered the gumbo to the house, Charlotte's big cat eyes were so bloodshot, it looked as though they were wrapped in tiny red fishnets. Yet she nodded and gave a small smile when I gave her the pot, almost as if she had been expecting it.

"She made it herself," I said.

"I know," she replied. "Where do you think I got my recipe?"

I honestly wasn't sure if what she said was true, but the moment revealed a deeper connection between the two women that came out only in the rarest of circumstances.

"You tell your mother that my family and I thank her for her kindness," she continued. "She's a woman of God, no matter how hard she tries to deny it."

These words echoed in my mind as I waited in the damp darkness for Charlotte to answer her door.

I heard shuffling from inside and then Charlotte appeared, pulling on her robe and rubbing her bleary eyes. She clicked on a small exterior bulb above the door that shot a shaft of light onto me like I was standing in a G-man's interrogation room. Behind her I could see she had just risen from the couch she slept on in the main room (she let her mother have the house's sole bedroom). Besides a few simple pieces of furniture, the only decoration in the main room consisted of framed portraits of two men. The first was the standard-issue print of Jesus Christ where he's posed kind of staring off to one side, looking all tan and healthy in his white robe. The second was an eight-by-ten glossy photograph of a handsome Negro man with neatly cropped hair and a thin mustache, who was wearing a sharp dark suit. At first I assumed it was a portrait of her late father as a young man. I later realized it was probably a photograph of Dr. Martin Luther King Jr.

"Louise?" she said.

"I n-need your help," I stammered.

Her eyes nervously shifted around and behind me, as if she were looking for the trouble that might have followed me there.

"Come inside."

She ushered me inside and closed and locked the door. I was still sweating and breathing heavily from the trip over.

"You've gotta help me."

"Help you . . . ?"

"Royce is at the house. . . ."

"Royce?"

"He's with Clem and they're both . . . you know . . ."

"They're both . . . ?"

"Going after her."

"Louise, I told you not to get involved with your mama and her men—"

"This is different. They're hurting her."

"She'll be all right, honey."

"No."

"Sometimes things can get a little rough, but your mama knows what she's doing."

"No. It's different. They're drunk."

"They're always drunk."

"But that's not all. They're gonna lynch him."

"Who's gonna lynch who?"

"Royce Burke and the Klan boys. They're gonna lynch Morgan."

"Morgan . . . ?"

"The man."

"Louise, you're not making any sense."

"The man who was staying at our place. They're gonna lynch him!"

"Why?"

"I don't know. They think he's an agitator."

"What kind of agitator?"

"You know, one of those who's trying to get the schools desegregated. He was at the school this morning. But he was just watching. He didn't do anything. And there was a fight. And then Royce Burke came looking for him with Clem Deneen. And when they found out he wasn't there, they went after her. But we've gotta find him. They're looking for him. All of them. They know his car. You've got to help him."

"I've gotta help him?" she said, incredulous.

"Yes. You've got to."

"Louise, honey, for such a smart girl, you can be as dumb as they come about some things."

Charlotte had never insulted me so directly. I could tell she really meant what she said, and the words stung.

"What do you mean?"

"Look at me, Louise. I mean really look."

She waited until my eyes locked on hers before continuing.

"I'm an old colored woman. You know what that means?"

"No," I said, not at all sure where she was going with this.

"That means I'm just one step above a stray dog to the law around here. Did you ever think of that? And what in the name of sweet Jesus do you think I could do to defend a white man from the Klan in the first place? They'd be more than happy to string an old piece of brown meat like me up in some tree, knowing that the law wouldn't even cut me down if they did. Did you ever think about that?"

"I'm trying to save him."

"There're plenty of people that need saving who parade right in front of your eyes every day, Louise. You ever think about those folks? I've known plenty of boys who've been lynched. You ever give them a thought? Ever think what it's like to be that little girl who's going to your school every day and having grown men throw bottles filled with piss at her? Have you ever really taken a look at what's going on over there at that school? That's what hell looks like, Louise. Hell right here in the Ninth Ward. Suddenly things matter to you just because you've got some puppy-love crush? Suddenly you grow a heart just because your hormones are kicking in? Maybe you and your mama aren't so different after all."

"She's not my mother," I whispered, too quietly for her to hear, afraid to actually let the words leak into the open air.

"What?" she asked.

"Nothing," I replied.

My mind raced in all directions but didn't land anywhere that could help Morgan—or me, for that matter. Tears ran down my cheeks, which seemed to soften her.

"Look, I'm sorry, honey. But there's nothing I can do. Your mother will be fine. And I'm sure that man will be fine too. And besides, if he really is in trouble with the Klan boys, my black face would only bring him more harm. You understand?"

I just stared at her, feeling utterly helpless. Charlotte had been my only real hope.

"Now, it's late," she continued. "You should be long in bed. I'll walk you back home." She turned back to retrieve her coat and shoes.

"No," I said. "Forget it."

I unlocked the door, stepped back outside, and grabbed my bike.

"Louise, hold on," Charlotte called after me. "It's too dark for you to be riding around like that."

I ignored her and pedaled away as fast as I could.

"Louise!" I heard her call after me again.

A light rain was falling, causing my glasses to

fog, but I didn't care. I felt utterly helpless and adrift. As I rode into the darkness, I didn't really fear anything, because I thought I had nothing more to lose. If some robber or boogeyman were to jump out of the bushes, he would just be saving me from my misery. If I crashed my bike, I would be brought to the temporary security of a hospital emergency room, where I would, at least for a while, belong. Emergency room doctors and nurses would have to care for me. At that moment I felt as if I didn't belong anywhere on Earth. Anywhere would have been better than going back to Rooms on Desire.

With no other reasonable option, I headed toward the only other place I thought might be able to lead me to Morgan.

CHAPTER 29

No lights shone from inside the apartment above Friendly Market on St. Claude. It must've been near midnight when I climbed the stairs to the second-floor landing. Without hesitating, I knocked loudly on the door. No reply. I knocked again, more insistently. After a moment I heard movement from within, and then the gruff voice of Morgan's brother, Michael.

"Look, if you're here to rob the place, you'd better back off! I've got a shotgun pointed right at the door."

"Mr. Miller?" I said.

"Who the hell . . . ?"

"Please, I need to talk to you."

The door, held by a chain, opened a crack, and his face peered out at me.

"What do you want?"

"I'm here about your brother."

"My brother?"

"Morgan. Morgan Miller. He's your brother, right?"

Michael unhooked the chain and opened the door, fully revealing himself. He was wearing blue-striped cotton pajamas and was, in fact, holding a .22-caliber rifle, not a shotgun. He held the slim weapon by his side like a cane. He looked smaller in his pajamas; his body seemed more bony and frail without the padding of his white coat; it was like seeing a turtle out of its shell.

"What about my brother?"

"He's in terrible trouble."

"Who are you?"

"Louise Collins."

"Who sent you here?"

"Nobody. He was staying at our inn. And they came looking for him."

"Who came looking for him?"

"Some Klan boys."

"The Ku Klux Klan?"

"Yes."

"How did they know he was staying with you?"

"I don't know. That's not important. They're bad men. They mean to lynch him."

"How do you know?"

"I heard them!"

Just then Michael's wife, Edie, the red-haired lady that I had seen in the market, approached from inside the apartment, tying on a pink terry-cloth bathrobe.

"Mickey, what's going on?" she said. She let out a funny little yelp of surprise when she saw me. "Who are you?"

"I need your help."

"She says Morgan's in trouble with the Klan."

"Your brother, Morgan? Did you know he was in town?" she asked her husband.

"Yes," he replied. "He came to see me."

"Why didn't you tell—"

"We'll talk about it later, Edie," he interrupted.

"You're soaking wet," she said to me. "Come inside."

"Look, I don't have time to come inside. You've got to help me find him."

"It's past midnight," he said. "You should be home in bed."

"But they have his license plate number. They're all looking for him. We've got to warn him. Please help me find him."

"I wouldn't have any idea where to look, little girl," he said. "Your guess is as good as mine."

"But don't you care? He's your brother. He looked up to you when you were growing up 'cause you were good at everything that he wasn't, like sports and girls. He said you were like a hero. And you played Treasure Island together. You were Long John Silver and he was Jim Hawkins. Don't you remember? And he's all alone now! He's all alone, now that his son got killed over in Korea and he and his wife split and he just wanted some family. That's all he wanted, some family! You've got a family. And he's got none! He's got no family! Can you imagine what it's like to wake up one day and have no family at all? No family!"

At this point the words bubbled and choked in my throat and I started sobbing hysterically. My body convulsed in heavy wet gasps that had a force beyond my control. Michael just stood staring at me, shocked both by my words and my hysteria. His wife knelt down and tried to console me.

"Look, honey, it's okay."

"It's not okay!" I sobbed.

"Just calm down," she said. "It's gonna be all right. It's gonna be all right. Just relax and tell me who your mama is. We'll give her a call. Okay?"

"My mother is dead!" I howled. "She's dead!"

The woman tried to reach out a hand to touch me, but I spun away from her grasp and ran back down the stairs.

I twisted down the dark stairwell and back out to the street. I dragged myself onto my bike and pedaled down St. Claude, feet pumping as hard as I could. My mind felt completely blank. I had no destination. No plan. Rain pelted my face, and my hair tangled in my mouth and glasses. Streetlights and neon whirled past my fogged vision.

Then the sudden flash of headlights.

The blare of a car horn.

Skidding tires on wet pavement.

And darkness.

CHAPTER 30

My back felt wet but warm against the pavement. My body was steaming. My chest heaved up and down, up and down. Nothing really hurt, but nothing felt right. My entire body was numb and prickly. The rain touched my eyelids, causing them to flicker open.

I saw the twisted frame of my bike lying a few feet away, illuminated by the headlights of a red milk delivery van. The driver of the van swung down from his seat and approached me. A few other people came toward me, as if my body were a magnet pulling all the night crawlers out of the shadows—a

Negro man in workman's coveralls on his way to or from the late shift; a white hobo wearing three pairs of pants, one over the other, a blond lady of the evening with deep red blotches of rouge on her cheeks, who was squeezed into a tight blue satin dress.

Out of the corner of my eye I saw the Bel Air approach and pull to a stop nearby. My heart sped up as I watched Morgan get out of the car and rush to my side. He waved the others back, saying that I needed room to breathe. He asked me if I was okay and I nodded yes, now I was okay. I would always be okay. My eyes flickered and closed, and then I was in his strong arms as he lifted me up and carried me to the car. I felt his warm breath on my face. I breathed deeply, hoping to catch some of his breath within mine.

He gently placed me in the backseat of the Bel Air. He produced a towel from the trunk and carefully wiped my face and arms. Then he folded the towel and placed it under my head. He told me to relax and not worry about anything. I did exactly as he said. He got behind the wheel and drove. I had no idea where we were going, but I knew it was going to be someplace safe and warm and that we'd be together. The radio was tuned to a Negro station, playing some sassy jazz with lots of horns. Morgan's arm rested across the top of the passenger seat and his hand tapped along to the bouncing rhythm. I smiled at the sight of his dancing hand and the back of his head nodding to the beat. I felt the tires whirring beneath us and glanced out the window at the rain and city streaking by. I turned back to Morgan. I could see one side of his face and the smiling crow's feet at the corner of his eye, which was focused on the road ahead, confidently guiding us through the storm. I closed my eyes. A moment later a bump in the road jarred me awake.

CHAPTER 31

When my eyes snapped open, my chest sank and the breath left my body as I took in my surroundings. I was still lying on the wet ground beside the twisted frame of my bike. The driver of the milk van, the hobo, the Negro workman, and the lady of the evening all approached me at once.

"Oh, damn it," the milk van driver muttered.

"You okay, girl?" the lady asked.

"You done hit her," the hobo said, pointing at the milk van driver. "I seen it. I seen it all. You hit her."

"She came out of nowhere," the driver replied. "Dere's no way I could've avoided her."

"Can you move, sugar?"

Good question. I slowly shifted different parts of my body, but everything seemed stiff, as if all my limbs had been frozen. After a few jerky movements my body came back alive. I saw my legs move before I felt them, then I felt my arms, torso, neck, hands, face, tongue, fingers, toes. I could feel everything. Thank the Lord. And I didn't perceive any real pain except for some scraped skin off my palms and knees. The lady offered me a hand up.

"Better not try to move her," the Negro workman suggested. "We should call somebody."

"You think you can get up, sugar?" the lady asked.

"She came out of nowhere," the milk van driver said again. "Right out of da dark."

I reached for the lady's hand, and she pulled me to my feet.

A police siren wailed in the distance, fast approaching.

"Son of a bitch," muttered the milk van driver.

"Here comes da law," chanted the hobo. "Dey gonna fix you good."

The lady of the evening quickly caressed my face and said, "Take care, sugar."

She slunk back into the shadows just as the police cruiser came into view and pulled to a stop beside my bike.

"You came out of nowhere," the van driver hissed at me as two officers emerged from the car. "I didn't do nothing wrong. You hear?"

"He done hit dis girl!" the hobo called as the police approached. "Done hit her with his van, he did. I saw da whole thing."

"All right, calm down, y'all," the police officer said.

"You okay, kid?" the other officer asked me, kneeling down to take a look.

"She came out of nowhere," the van driver piped up. "I drive this route every single day. Never had a ticket in my life."

"Dat what happened?" the officer asked.

"I didn't see it happen." The Negro workman shrugged.

"Dere was nothing to see," the van driver said. "She came out of nowhere."

"He done hit her! I saw it!" the hobo chimed in.

"Shut your trap," said the first officer.

"Are you okay, kid?" the second officer asked me again. "Looks like you've got a couple of scrapes."

"I'm okay," I said, surprised by the sound of my own voice.

"What happened?"

"He didn't do anything," I said, nodding at the van driver. "I wasn't looking where I was going is all."

"What are you doing riding around at dis hour?" he asked me.

I didn't respond.

"Does your mama know where you are?" the first officer asked.

I didn't respond.

"Look, kid, we know you can talk," he said.

"We're not trying to get you in trouble," the second one said. "We just want to get you home where you belong."

CHAPTER 32

The short ride in the back of the police car helped snap me back to the harsh reality I was facing. Nothing can make your brain stand up at attention like fear. I wasn't sure what I'd discover when we got back to the house. Would Royce and Clem still be there? Was my mother okay? If she was okay, I knew I'd be facing some serious trouble. I had just destroyed my most expensive possession—my bike. If only I had sustained a decent injury, even something as small as a broken finger, I might've been granted some leniency. With just a couple of scraped knees to my credit, I had good reason to expect every known punishment short of the death penalty.

When we arrived back at Rooms on Desire, the two police officers escorted me to the door. They knocked once, but no one answered. They knocked again, even louder. The tension rose as we waited. Finally, Charlotte Dupree answered the door. She must have come looking for me after my hysterical visit to her house. A wave of relief swept through me at the sight of her. Before any words were exchanged, I ran into Charlotte's arms and she held me tightly against her body.

"It's okay, baby," Charlotte said, eyeing the police suspiciously.

"Are da girl's parents around?" one of the officers asked.

"Her mother's asleep," she said.

"Well, wake her up. We need to talk to her."

"She's sick," Charlotte replied. "She needs to rest."

"Don't you give us any lip," he replied curtly. "We found dis girl lying on the side of the road. She got hit by a van."

"Are you hurt, baby?" Charlotte asked me.

I shook my head no.

She knelt down and examined my skinned knees.

"We'll get those bobos all cleaned up right quick," she said.

"We still need to talk to one of her parents."

"Look, it's past midnight and everyone's asleep," Charlotte pleaded. "Couldn't you just come back—"

"It's okay, Charlotte," my mother's voice called from the shadows at the top of the stairs.

"You da girl's mother?" one of them asked.

"Yeah," she responded. "She's mine."

"We need to speak with you, ma'am."

She slowly descended the stairs. As she came into the light, I gasped. She had suffered minor cuts and bruises from Royce before, but nothing like this. I barely recognized her. Her entire face had been transformed into a swollen red mask. One side of her face had grown significantly larger than the other. The skin around and under her left eye was severely bruised a brownish-purple color. The white of the eye was flooded with blood, so the whole eye was a dark red. Her right cheek had a massive raised bruise, so it looked like she had a small baseball lodged beside her teeth and gums. She walked slowly and deliberately, as if any sudden movement would cause her more pain.

"What da hell happened to you?" one of the officers asked.

"Had an accident. Fell down these stairs."

"All dat from falling down some stairs?" the other officer asked doubtfully.

"I've never been Ginger Rogers," my mother quipped.

"You should see a doctor," the other officer said.

"I just need rest."

She winced in pain as she came to the bottom step and moved toward us.

"You sure dere isn't anything you need to report to us? Or anybody?"

"Not unless you want to arrest the stairs or my clumsy feet."

"Well, your family had quite a bad night. Your

daughter had a little accident too," the first officer said.

"She's fine, but her bike got wrecked," the other added.

"She really shouldn't have been riding around at dis hour," the first continued.

"She went to borrow some rubbing alcohol from a neighbor for me," she lied. "Come here, Louise. Let me take a look at you."

I disengaged from Charlotte and slowly moved toward her. I saw her one clear eye watching me closely. When I was beside her, she stared at me. Her good eye was filled with tears that did not spill over down her face. She touched my hair, brushing a few strands out of my eyes, and then she let her hand come to rest on my shoulder.

"Thank you for returning her, officers," she said. "But now I think we could all use some rest."

"You sure dere's nothing y'all need to report, ma'am?" one of them asked her again.

She paused a moment before responding. For that moment I truly thought she might say something

about Royce and Clem, or even Morgan. But she
didn't.

"Yes. I'm sure," she said. "Good night, gentle-
men."

"Just keep her off da streets at night, okay?" the
other one said, nodding to me.

After they left, my mother kept her hand on my
shoulder for a long moment. I felt her grip tighten,
yet I wasn't sure if she was applying more pressure
as some sign of reprimand or affection, or to hold
herself up. After I heard the police car drive away, I
waited for her to explode, but she never did. She
released her grip on my shoulder.

"Help me back up the stairs," she said to neither
of us in particular. "Please."

Charlotte and I flanked her and helped guide
her back up the stairs to her room. It was a long,
painful journey.

"Okay, just take it nice and slow," Charlotte
advised.

With each step her leg muscles jerked and tightened. When we finally got to the door of her room,

I could see she had worked up a sweat. She turned to me. Her eyes looked at me with a strange sadness, as if she were trying to remember something and forget something at the same time. She reached out her hand and gently touched the side of my face with her fingertips.

"Go to bed, Louise."

And then she disappeared inside her room.

CHAPTER 33

The next morning she did not emerge from her room at her usual time to join the other ladies down at the school. In fact she stayed in her room with the door closed the entire day. Charlotte and I went back to our business-as-usual routine of taking care of things around the house and tending to Mr. Landroux. We didn't talk much. There didn't seem to be much to say. Charlotte brought my mother a pot of tea in the morning and a pitcher of lime juleps in the afternoon. After she returned to the kitchen with the empty pitcher, I asked, "Is she okay?" Charlotte shrugged. "She isn't talking much. But the swelling's gone down a bit."

I spent the better part of the day watching and waiting for Morgan's brother, Michael, to show up and help me find Morgan. Whenever a car passed the house, I was sure it was him. But no one ever stopped. In fact, no one came by the house at all that day except the postman to deliver the mail and Charlotte's friend Julie, who dropped off a small pot of her homemade turtle soup at the back door. How could Michael be so heartless? I wondered. Maybe he just didn't believe me.

Before Charlotte left that night, she put the pot of fiery rice and cheese back in the oven.

"Try to get her to eat something," she said. Then she echoed the words my mother had said to me three years earlier. "A full stomach is one of the only things that can truly lessen sorrow." I was left to wonder who actually had the insight first.

At seven thirty I ventured upstairs with a plate of rice and softly knocked on the door.

"Are you hungry?" I asked through the door.

"No," she said. Her voice sounded distant even

though she was just a few feet away behind the door.

"Can I get you anything?"

"No," she said. "Thank you."

I retreated back downstairs, fed myself, brought Mr. Landroux his dinner tray, and then closed up the house for the night. Once I tucked myself in bed, I knew I'd have no chance of sleeping. I was way too stirred up. I tried to finish *Jane Eyre*, but the words seemed to scramble in my head as soon as they got past my eyes. So I moved on to something lighter. I flipped through an old issue of *Screenland* with Debbie Reynolds on the cover, but I couldn't interest myself in even the juiciest bits of celebrity gossip: "Robert Wagner and Natalie Wood Share Their Secrets for Marital Bliss," "Connie Francis Reveals How She First Learned About Boys," "Bill Holden's Got a Secret!" Nothing. I tossed the magazine aside and just lay in bed, hoping that sleep would come, but it didn't.

All I could think of was Morgan. I wondered if he was awake or asleep, safe or in danger.

Then, sometime well past midnight but before

dawn, I heard my mother finally emerge from her room and walk downstairs. She didn't turn on any lights or the radio. Maybe she was hungry and had gone to fix herself something. I quietly got out of bed and slowly tiptoed down the front hall steps. I paused at the bottom of the stairs and scanned the front of the house. No lights were on in the Music Hall, so I assumed she was in the kitchen. But then I saw her silhouette illuminated by the moonlight shining through the front windows.

She sat at the old piano and ran her fingers over the keys without striking any notes. Her head was slightly bent, and her eyes seemed to be focused on a point on the music stand, as if she were trying to decipher some invisible piece of sheet music. I watched her for a moment in silence, until she lifted her head as if she'd heard me breathing. I instinctively stepped back.

"Louise?" she called into the dark.

"Yeah," I answered after a moment of hesitation.

"Come here."

I walked over and stood beside the piano, where

I could finally get a good look at her. The swelling
in her face had gone down, so it was back to nearly
its normal size, but the color of her black eye had
deepened and there was still a noticeable mark on
her cheek.

"Can't sleep?" she asked.

"No."

"Neither can I."

"Can I get you something?" I asked.

"No. Have a seat," she said, indicating a space on
the piano bench beside her. I sat.

"Do you know where this piano came from?"
she asked.

She had spun literally dozens of yarns about the
piano's origins over the years, so I had no idea which
one, if any, held a kernel of truth. Was it a gift to her
grandmother from Jefferson Davis? Did her father
win it by eating sixteen pecan pies in a contest at the
Louisiana State Fair? Was it the sole valuable possession her family had rescued from Ireland when
they escaped the potato famine?

"No," I replied. "I don't."

272 ROBERTROBERT SHARENOW

"I bought it," she said. I detected a decent measure of pride in her voice. "Bought it with my own money just after we moved here. When I was a little girl, I always wished we had our own piano. I learned to play on my cousin Imogene's upright, and I always resented her because her parents could afford one and mine couldn't. I was a much better player than Imogene. I thought she didn't deserve to have a piano in her house, the way she used to butcher 'Für Elise.' Beethoven must've been rolling in his grave every time she got near the ivories. Some kids had to be forced to take piano lessons, but not me. I always wanted to play. And I was good, too.

"Piano music always seemed romantic to me. I used to listen to all the radio serials when I was a little girl. Whenever there was a party in one of the stories, there was always someone playing the piano in the background. It didn't matter if the party was at a penthouse apartment in Manhattan or a grand plantation in Georgia. I always dreamed of going to one of those parties.

"After your father ran off and we moved back here, I promised myself that I'd get a piano to cheer myself up and bring a little bit of class to this place. I worked as a barmaid at Pat O'Brien's on Bourbon Street three nights a week for nearly a year to help pay for the thing. I'll never forget the day the delivery men dropped it off. A bunch of neighbors came out to admire the piano and give me little compliments about my good taste and how I was really getting the place in shape. But then once it got here, I knew right away I'd made a mistake. No one we ever have staying here really wants to hear someone play the piano. They either want peace and quiet or to go raise hell in the Quarter."

"Not a whole lot of music lovers," I said.

"No, not a whole lot," she agreed with a small chuckle.

We fell into a moment of silence.

"I heard you sing the other night," I said.

"Did you?"

"It's a pretty song. 'Do You Know What It Means to Miss New Orleans.'"

"I always thought so."

"Ricky Nelson sings the same song, you know."

"I haven't heard his version."

"It's all right. You sing it better."

"You really think so?"

"Yes."

"Thank you, Louise. You know, I always meant to give you lessons. . . . There are a whole bunch of things I meant to do for you, but . . ."

She never finished the sentence.

"I think we'd both better get some sleep," she finally said, "or we'll both be zombies come morning."

She still moved with discomfort. I let her lean a hand on my shoulder and helped her back up to her room. When we got to the top of the landing, she bent down and gave me a small kiss on the cheek, which took me by surprise.

"You're a good girl, Louise."

Then she retreated into her room and closed the door.

When I got back into bed, I felt an unusual

patch of warmth spread out across my cheek where she had kissed me. I closed my eyes and fell asleep almost instantly.

That day, once again, my mother did not emerge from her room at the usual hour. I wondered if she was going to miss another day of cheerleading. She'd never missed a morning with the ladies until the previous day. Was she afraid to face everybody with her injured face? Or was she having doubts about being out there protesting in the first place? Maybe something Morgan had said had gotten through to her.

I was in the kitchen preparing Mr. Landroux's breakfast tray with Charlotte when there was a knock at the front door. Charlotte's hands were full of flour, so I answered it. When I opened the door, I found Nitty Babcock holding a small hand mirror up to her face while she picked at her front tooth with her fingernail.

"Oh, morning, dear," she said, returning the mirror to her purse. "Your mother home?"

"She's still sleeping," I replied.

"Well, let her know da folks from CBS News who were supposed to come by da school on Monday are actually coming by today. Lena Witt heard from her sister, who works at da Chamberlain hotel, and dat's where they're staying. Da film crew, dat is. Shame dey didn't stay here, isn't it, girl? Well, anyway, if she wants to get a good spot, she'd better get down dere early. Lots of da girls are already out dere."

A moment after Nitty departed, my mother's door opened and she emerged fully dressed in one of her best ensembles, a green polka-dot number with the matching faux alligator shoes and handbag. Her expert makeup job covered nearly all the damage to her face. Her cheek still looked slightly swollen and her eye was still stained dark red, but other than that you really wouldn't have noticed anything. She walked down the stairs to where I stood in the entry hall. She seemed to be moving with minimal discomfort. She checked her lipstick in the mirror in the front hall and reapplied it to her bottom lip.

"Nitty just came by . . ." I said.

"I heard her," she replied.

"Are you going to the school?"

"Yes."

I felt a bitter twinge of disappointment.

"Don't forget to tell Charlotte that Mr. Bayonne is coming by sometime this morning to look at the boiler," she continued. "But don't let him do anything until I find out the price. Those boys can gouge you."

She moved to the door.

"Don't go," I said, barely above a whisper.

She paused and turned to look at me.

"Excuse me?"

"I said don't go."

She stared at me for a long moment.

"Don't worry, Louise."

And with that she was out the door. What did she mean, "Don't worry, Louise?" Don't worry about what? Don't worry about her? Don't worry about Morgan? Don't worry about Ruby Bridges? Don't worry about my busted bicycle? Don't worry about ever going to school again? Don't worry about not having a real mama or daddy? Don't worry about my crooked bottom teeth? Don't worry about not having any friends? Don't worry about Communist spies? Don't worry about Mr. Bayonne quoting a high price to fix the boiler? I was worried about everything. What was she talking about, telling me not to worry?

CHAPTER 34

I followed her out the door and trailed her at a discreet distance. I think she knew I was following her, but she never turned back to look my way. When we arrived at William Frantz Elementary School, everything looked the same and everything looked different. To my eye the entire scene seemed more menacing, like I could feel the violence pulsing under everyone's skin, ready to burst out. The typical gathering of good old boys, journalists, FBI agents, police officers, neighborhood kids, random spectators, and of course the Cheerleaders—all were in position around the school, awaiting the arrival of Ruby Bridges. I half expected, or hoped, to see Morgan drive up in the Bel Air and take his position opposite the Cheerleaders, but he didn't.

There may have been a few more people than usual because CBS News had in fact sent a crew to do a story on the protests. A CBS reporter and cameraman were set up on the sidewalk near the pack of Cheerleaders, interviewing Ada Munson. "Dis is our school," she said into the microphone. "And we're gonna be out here as long as it takes to get da niggers out."

Most of the rest of the Cheerleaders were gathered around Antoinette Lawrence, who held a copy of the morning edition of *The Times-Picayune*, which featured an article titled "Cheerleaders Plan Fund-Raising Trip to Ole Miss." Antoinette read highlights to the group: "'The ladies of the Ninth Ward say dey are not giving in to integration without a fight. Dis weekend dey intend to spread their fund-raising efforts to pay for a new segregated school in Mississippi. . . .'"

My mother didn't appear to be paying any attention to what anyone was saying. She just seemed to be
looking around, taking it all in. Perhaps she, too, was
hoping that Morgan would drive up in the Bel Air.
Nitty Babcock caught sight of her and approached.

"Pauline, you missed da crowd shot."

"Huh?" she replied.

"Da crowd shot. Da CBS cameraman lined us all
up and got a shot of everyone holding their signs
and yelling. . . . What happened to your eye?"

"Had an accident," she replied.

"Well, try to turn to favor your left eye if da
camera swings our way again. Dis is a national
broadcast. . . ."

While Nitty prattled on, something gave my
mother pause. I saw her eyes narrow as she focused on the back of the newspaper Antoinette
Lawrence was holding. Something about a black-
and-white photograph on the bottom of the page
caught her eye. I saw it too and felt my stomach
instantly tense into a dozen knots. Nitty Babcock
had a copy of the same paper tucked under her arm.

My mother plucked it from her without asking.

"Hey, dat's mine," she said.

"Hush up," my mother snapped.

"Just let me have it back when you're done. I want de article for my scrapbook, okay, Pauline? Pauline?"

She ignored Nitty and flipped open to the page with the photograph. The stark black-and-white image depicted a car engulfed in flames sitting next to a burning cross on the side of a road at night. A small group of state police and firefighters watched from a distance, their faces alive in the fire. One of the policeman looked like he might have been smiling. The color ran out of her face as my mother read the article to herself. I didn't get to read the full article until later that day.

Burning Car Discovered on Rt. 46

by Stephen Mouledoux, *Times-Picayune* Staff

At 11:14 P.M. on Tuesday night, state police and firefighters responding to an anonymous call discovered a burning car on Rt. 46, two miles outside of Meraux. A large wooden cross was also burning nearby when the police arrived.

The car, a 1956 Chevrolet Bel Air, had New York license plates and is registered to Morgan Ira Miller of West 81st Street in New York.

There was no sign of the driver in the car or in the vicinity. An empty gas can was discovered in some bushes nearby. By the time the fire trucks arrived, it was too late to salvage the vehicle.

Fire Chief Remy Boncoeur commented, "It looks like the thing was doused in gas and someone just lit her up like a candle. There's no way to save a car that's been torched like that."

The police were not commenting on any suspects or motives for the incident and were quick to dispel any speculation about who might be involved.

State police Sergeant Joseph Lefevre said, "When you see a burning cross, most people think of the Klan, but at this point we have no leads, so we're not going to point any fingers." The state police are currently looking for any leads as to who set the blaze and the whereabouts of the driver.

Royce crept up behind my mother while she was reading. "It's too bad you didn't come," he snarled quietly in her ear. She jumped slightly at the sound of his voice. "You could've brought da marshmallows." She turned to face him. He winked and walked back to stand with Clem and some of the other good old boys who were leaning on a row of cars parked nearby.

Just then, the crowd noise swelled and the CBS camera was repositioned as the sedan carrying Ruby Bridges approached the school. Ada Munson began leading the chanting. "Two, four, six, eight, We don't want to integrate!" Bea Williams positioned her Negro baby doll in its coffin. The car pulled to a stop, and Ruby Bridges emerged wearing one of those blindingly white dresses with a white bow in her hair. Once her bodyguards were in place, they marched up toward the front entrance of the school, and the howling escalated. A few rotten eggs landed near Ruby's feet, and the yolk splattered her neatly polished shoes. She barely flinched and never broke stride.

Charlotte's words echoed in my head—"That's what hell looks like, Louise. Hell right here in the Ninth Ward"—until they were drowned out by the rush of all of the voices from the crowd mixed together.

"Two, four, six, eight, We don't want to integrate!"

"We're gonna lynch your daddy!"

"Go home, pickaninny!"

"Don't eat your lunch today, unless you want a poison sandwich."

"God hates integration!"

"Here, nigger, nigger, nigger, nigger . . ."

"Da righteous will prevail!"

My mother didn't join in the chanting. She just stared, her eyes trained on Ruby Bridges as if she were really looking at her for the first time. Her gaze followed Ruby up the steps leading to the school, and then she turned back and scanned the howling protestors. Her eyes came to rest on me, standing on the outskirts of the crowd. We stared at each other for a long moment.

Finally she came over to me and took my hand, and we walked away.

And she never went back.

Acts of courage come in all shapes and sizes. Sometimes what seems like a small moment to one person constitutes an unprecedented act of bravery for another. What my mother did may have looked small and ordinary to some people. But I knew that it was a true act of courage.

As we moved away from the school, the noise of the crowd receded. I couldn't recall the last time she had held my hand. Her fingers were soft and yet strong. I felt her grip tighten, and it struck me that I was gently being pulled away, that she was actually leading me somewhere. My heart rose up in my chest, and for a few moments it felt as if I were actually floating just a few inches off the sidewalk. I gripped her hand tightly the entire walk home, and for the first time in my life I was proud of her.

Morgan's body was never found. Over the years I've tried my best not to imagine where it must've ended up. I've managed to keep one specific image of him trapped in my memory. It was the very first moment I laid eyes on him, stepping out of his car, stretching his arms over his head and letting the sun fall on his face, like he didn't have a care in the world.

I'd like to say that my mother did a complete reversal and joined the pro-integration forces and marched for civil rights, but she didn't. I guess sometimes small steps matter just as much as grand gestures. She was one less voice shouting down the winds of change, and that felt important—at least it did to me.

From that day onward, she still drank her lime juleps. She was still short-tempered, vain, and a bit of a loudmouth. But she was no longer a Cheerleader. And she was my mother. She was my mother.

By the spring of 1961 several white students, including me, returned to class at William Frantz Elementary School. Gradually the protests diminished. The following September Ruby Bridges and several other Negro students entered an integrated second-grade class. And there were no Cheerleaders or any other protestors outside the school.

Although this is a work of fiction, many of the situations depicted are based on actual historical events. All the characters are fictional with the exception of John Steinbeck and Ruby Bridges. In writing this book, I relied upon the work of many historians. Yet I am most deeply indebted to Dr. Juliette Landphair, whose doctoral thesis on the Ninth Ward of New Orleans provided invaluable insights into the neighborhood, its people, and their reactions to the integration of their public schools. Dr. Landphair also shared with me hundreds of pages of previously classified FBI reports on the Cheerleaders and the anti-integration movement. I thank her for both her outstanding scholarship and her personal generosity.

ACKNOWLEDGMENTS

I want to thank my editor and publisher, Laura Geringer, who believed in the book from the very beginning and has been an incredible creative partner every step of the way. My agent, Maria Massie, is an invaluable advisor, champion, friend, and therapist.

I would also like to thank those who served as readers, critics, and spiritual supporters throughout my writing process, particularly Martin Curland, Alexandra Tolk, Christine Gomez, Nancy Dubuc, Scott Brody, David Lawrence, Sam Mettler, Louise

Maxwell, Scott Klass, Steven Nathanson, Dan Miller, Jill Santopolo, and Lindsey Alexander. I'm also deeply indebted to Bob Miller, Elizabeth Beier, and my lawyer, Lisa Davis, who explained the facts of publishing life to me.

My daughters, Annabelle and Olivia, inspire me every day with their love, humor, and fresh insights into the world. They also proved to me that we are truly born color-blind. Most of all, I want to thank my wife, Stacey. In addition to being my soul mate, Stacey is a brilliantly insightful editor and writer. She is always my first and most important reader.

MY MOTHER
THE CHEERLEADER

EXTRAS

A Letter from Robert Sharenow

Dear Reader,

I thought I'd take the opportunity to introduce the "Extras" portion of this book and explain some of the background of how I came to write *My Mother the Cheerleader*.

Since September 11, 2001, we've been living in very challenging and confusing times. Often it's hard to make sense of what goes on in the world. In the wake of the attack on the World Trade Center, I found myself drawn to reading about the civil rights movement. For me, those were times when there was a clear moral right and wrong, and good and courageous people like Ruby Bridges helped change the course of our nation for the better. I found comfort in these stories. So much has been written about the heroes of that struggle, but very little covers the events from the other side.

While researching for the book, I created my own timeline of the civil rights movement to put the events that happened in New Orleans into a broader historical context. I've included an enhanced version of the timeline for this edition of the book along with an interview I did about the genesis of the novel and writing in general. And for those of you interested in writing historical fiction, I've also brainstormed some tips that will help you get started.

I hope you find the information useful.

All the Best,
Robert Sharenow

An Interview with Robert Sharenow

Why did you write *My Mother the Cheerleader*?

The writing of my book was directly inspired by John Steinbeck's *Travels with Charley*, a nonfiction account of a cross-country driving trip Steinbeck made with his poodle, Charley. The book climaxes with a visit to New Orleans to witness the spectacle of the Cheerleaders protesting the integration of the city's public schools in the Ninth Ward.

I was reading *Travels with Charley* around the time that my first daughter was born. Becoming a parent was the most transforming experience of my adult life. To me, it seemed to be an experience that cut across all racial, social, and religious barriers. So when I read Steinbeck's book, I was astonished at the savagery of the Cheerleaders toward Ruby Bridges. These were, after all, mothers. How could they treat a child so horribly when all she was trying to do was go to school? What kind of person would make death threats to a six-year-old girl?

I had always admired Steinbeck's writing because of his humanity. He wrote about downtrodden people who typically didn't get written about (*The Grapes of Wrath, Tortilla Flat, Cannery Row, The Pearl,* etc.). I was disappointed by his one-dimensional portrayal of the Cheerleaders. He failed to see any humanity in them, which seemed to contradict his point of view as a writer. Steinbeck didn't provide any insights as to their motivations—their reasons for thinking and behaving as they did. I really set out to write the book to explore what causes people to hate like that.

You weren't born until after the time the book takes place. How did you go about researching the time period?

I really got sucked in to the research. I read a stack of books on the civil rights movement. I also befriended a wonderful historian who is an expert in the field, who helped direct me to the best sources. She shared with me hundreds of pages of FBI reports on the Cheerleaders that were incredibly helpful.

You aren't from Louisiana originally—did you ever live there, or spend time there?

I'm originally from the Boston area, but I've visited New Orleans and I really fell in love with the city. It's got such a unique culture. The Ninth Ward, where the action of the book takes place, was one of the areas hardest hit by Hurricane Katrina, so almost no one remains who was there in 1960.

Do you have a favorite character in your book?

That's a very difficult question. I love all of my main

characters. I guess Pauline, the mother, is the most interesting to me, because she is the most unlike me.

Was it hard to write convincingly from the point of view of a girl?

Surprisingly—no. In fact, that was one of the easiest parts of the writing. Once I discovered Louise's voice, the writing became much easier. I grew up in a house with two older sisters, my wife and I have lived together for almost twenty years, and now we have two amazing daughters, so I'm used to being surrounded by females.

How long did it take you to write *My Mother the Cheerleader*?

I researched the subject for several years and was writing and rewriting for about two years.

What were some of your childhood ambitions? Did you always want to be a writer, or did your writing career come as a surprise?

On some level, I've always wanted to be a writer (although the desire wasn't fully expressed until I got out of college). I've always been awed by books and have been drawn to libraries and bookstores. But for a while I aspired to be a cartoonist and when I was in college I created a comic strip for our school paper. To me, writing a comic strip is one of the hardest creative disciplines because you have so little space and so few words to convey your characters and story. Charles M. Schulz, who created the comic strip *Peanuts*, has always been a hero of mine. With just a few spare lines of ink, he was able to communicate an entire universe of characters and stories representing so many aspects of the human experience. Charlie Brown, Lucy, Linus, and Snoopy are amazingly dimensional and real to me.

What's your writing routine?

I have a full-time job and two amazing kids; so most of the writing I do takes place in the early morning. When I'm working on a project, I generally get up at 5:15 A.M. and work until 7:00 A.M., when my wife and kids get up. I also travel a lot for my job, so I've learned to write on airplanes and at night in hotel rooms. It's ironic, but I think my writing improved when my life got more complicated and I had less time to write. Because my time is so limited, I really have to believe in what I'm working on.

Do you have a favorite place to write?

I prefer to work in my office. But for me, one of the keys to being able to finish projects was learning how to write in almost any environment. Given my current lifestyle, I can't afford to wait until I am on a mountaintop retreat or in some soundproof sanctuary to get my writing done.

What is your other job, when you're not writing?

I currently have a great job as head of nonfiction programming for A&E network. I started as a television writer and producer, so I've had the chance to work with some amazing people and a very diverse array of characters, from legendary rocker Gene Simmons to master illusionist Criss Angel. Being exposed to so many different people from all levels of society has definitely given me insights into the world that I use in my writing.

How does the writing process compare with the process of working in television?

Producing television shows and writing novels are vastly different experiences. TV is completely collaborative. For every show you watch, it takes a small army of people to get it on the air, including producers, editors, camera people, writers, sound engineers, composers, and musicians. If any one of the people on that chain doesn't do their job well, the final product suffers.

On the other hand, novel writing is a solitary endeavor. In some ways that's great because the author is more in control of the work (at least in the first draft). Having a great editor is extremely important, too. But I never even met my editor face-to-face until after the editing of the manuscript was complete. I will say that having strong writing and storytelling skills is the most important part of the TV producing process.

What were your favorite books when you were a teenager?

To Kill a Mockingbird made a big impression on me (and influenced the writing of my novel). I read William Styron's *Sophie's Choice* when I was in high school and it's still one of my favorite novels. I also went through a big Kurt Vonnegut phase when I was in high school. It broke my heart when he passed away. He always had such a young spirit in his writing; it was hard to imagine him getting old and sick. In one of his final interviews, he said, "The function of the artist is to make people like life better than they have before. When I've been asked if I've seen that done, I say, 'Yes, the Beatles did it.'" I love that quote, being a fan of both Vonnegut and the Beatles.

What advice would you give an aspiring writer?

Write whatever you are passionate about. Don't try to write what you think is cool or what you think you're supposed to write. I had no direct connection to the subjects of my book. I'm not a thirteen-year-old girl. I'm not from New Orleans. And I wasn't even born when the book takes place. Yet I was inspired to write that story.

Tips for Writing Historical Fiction

I've always been a history buff. For me, there's something magical about getting lost in another time and place. Here are some tips to help you discover the past and bring it alive in your writing.

The Library Is a Time Machine—The most easily accessible and abundant resource for accessing the past is your local library. Read as many books about your subject as possible—everything from history books to biographies and even other novels written about and during your time period.

Primary Sources Rule—Histories and biographies can be very useful in research, but they are what are known as "secondary sources." You should always try to track down "primary sources." A primary source is something that was created during the time period itself, such as a newspaper, magazine, historical document, movie or radio broadcast, or a firsthand account from someone who actually lived through the moment and recorded an oral history, interview, or autobiography. Historians and biographers build their works by examining primary sources, so you should always try to go directly to a primary source when possible, so you get an unfiltered view.

Watch TV and Movies—There are scores of documentaries on nearly every subject you can imagine. Just like books, when it comes to video artifacts there are primary sources and secondary sources. A documentary is a secondary source while a movie or radio/TV broadcast from the time period is a primary source. Try listening to the radio broadcast of the explosion of the Hindenburg and then read an article about it. You'll see that there's nothing quite as dramatic as listening to the harrowed broadcaster as he tries to describe the tragedy happening right before his eyes. Photographs can also be a great primary source. Mathew Brady's photographs provide some of the most vivid documents of the Civil War.

Listen to Old Music—Music is a great way to understand the past. Try tracking down the music from your time period and then create a top-ten list for each of your characters.

Eat Old-Fashioned Food—I love to eat. When I was researching *My Mother the Cheerleader*, I experimented with cooking and eating authentic recipes from New Orleans. Taste is an underrated sense and can be a very powerful tool in setting a mood in your writing. I worked as a producer for the History Channel and we once did a special on the Lewis and Clark expedition and what they ate to survive on their journey. I don't remember too many specific details about Lewis or Clark, but I'll never forget the fatty, gamey flavor of grilled beaver tail (I do not recommend it).

Live One Day in the Past—Turn off your cell phone, shut down your computer, unplug the TV, and try to live one day as a person would have in the past. If you are writing about a time before the invention of the automobile, try walking or riding your bike to all the places you'd need to go to survive (supermarket, doctor's office, school, etc.). If you are writing about a time before electricity, live by candlelight.

Historical Tourism—If you want to find out just how cold it was for Washington's soldiers during their winter in Valley Forge, go visit Valley Forge in December and stand outside for a few hours. Obviously, this type of travel can be prohibitively expensive, but it's extremely helpful to experience the sights, sounds, and smells of a place firsthand. However, novels are acts of the imagination, so don't feel too bad if you can't take your dream trip. Feel free to write about whatever you want even if you can't get there.

Don't Fear the Elderly (They Won't Bite)—Perhaps the best way to understand history is to speak to someone who actually lived through it. I'm currently working on a novel set in Nazi Germany in the 1930s and I've had the privilege of speaking to several people who were there. Nothing has brought the past to life more for me than having conversations with these survivors. They have been more than happy to share their time and memories with me. Living witnesses are a historian's most precious gift.

A Civil Rights Timeline

1863
President Lincoln issues the Emancipation Proclamation freeing all slaves in places still in rebellion against the Union.

1865
Confederate troops surrender at Appomattox, ending the Civil War.

The Thirteenth Amendment to the Constitution is adopted, abolishing slavery.

1866
The Ku Klux Klan, a group advocating white supremacy, is formed by veterans of the Confederate army.

1870
The Fifteenth Amendment is added to the U.S. Constitution, barring racial discrimination in voting.

1875
Congress passes a civil rights act granting equal rights in jury duty service and public accommodations.

1896

The Supreme Court hands down the *Plessy v. Ferguson* decision, which establishes the "separate but equal" doctrine, justifying segregation, including in the public schools.

1909

The National Congress on the Negro is held. This ultimately leads to the founding of the National Association for the Advancement of Colored People (NAACP).

1948

President Harry Truman outlaws segregation in the U.S. military.

1954

The Supreme Court hands down the *Brown v. Board of Education of Topeka* decision, which overturns the separate but equal doctrine established by *Plessy v. Ferguson* and declares segregation of public schools unconstitutional.

Fourteen-year-old Emmett Till is brutally beaten and killed for allegedly whistling at a white woman. Till's death becomes a rallying point of the civil rights movement.

1955

African-American heroine Rosa Parks refuses to move to the back of a Montgomery, Alabama, bus as required by a city ordinance. Her arrest triggers a boycott, which leads to the bus segregation ordinance being declared unconstitutional.

The Federal Interstate Commerce Commission bans segregation on interstate trains and buses.

Martin Luther King, Jr., and others establish the Southern Christian Leadership Conference, which becomes a major force in the civil rights movement. King serves as the group's first president.

1957
The governor of Arkansas uses National Guard troops to block nine black students from attending a Little Rock high school. President Eisenhower sends in federal troops to ensure compliance with a court order to integrate the school. The students come to be known as the Little Rock Nine.

1960
Four black college students begin sit-ins at the lunch counter of a Greensboro, North Carolina, restaurant, protesting the restaurant's policy of not serving black patrons.

Students at Shaw University in Raleigh, North Carolina, form the Student Non-Violent Coordinating Committee (also known as SNCC).

First grader Ruby Bridges becomes the first African-American student in New Orleans' William Frantz Elementary School. The Cheerleaders' protests against her enrollment draw national attention to the cause of school desegregation.

1961
Freedom Riders protesting segregation depart from Washington, D.C., traveling by buses into southern states.

1962
Riots erupt at the University of Mississippi over the enrollment of James Meredith, the school's first black student. President Kennedy sends in federal troops to quell the riots.

The Supreme Court rules that segregation is unconstitutional in all transportation facilities.

After being arrested during an antisegregation protest in Alabama, Martin Luther King composes his famous "Letter from Birmingham Jail," which argues that civil disobedience is justified when defying unjust laws.

1963
Civil rights activist Medgar Evers is shot and killed by a member of the Ku Klux Klan.

On August 28, 1963, Martin Luther King delivers the "I

Have a Dream" speech to more than 200,000 people at the March on Washington.

Ku Klux Klan members bomb a church in Birmingham, Alabama, killing four young black girls.

1964
The Twenty-fourth Amendment to the Constitution is ratified, making poll taxes illegal. Poll taxes had been imposed during Reconstruction to prevent people from voting.

Congress passes the Civil Rights Act, declaring discrimination based on race illegal. The act passes despite a seventy-five-day filibuster by prosegregationists.

Three civil rights workers—one black, two Jewish—disappear in Mississippi after being stopped for speeding. Their dead bodies are found buried six weeks later.

1965
A march is held from Selma to Montgomery, Alabama, to demand protection for voting rights after two civil rights workers were slain earlier in the year. This series of three marches includes "Bloody Sunday," in which marchers are attacked by police with hoses and tear gas, drawing national sympathy to the fight for civil rights.

On February 21, 1965, Malcolm X is assassinated while

giving a speech in New York City.

In August, six days of rioting erupt in the Watts neighborhood of Los Angeles.

The National Voting Rights Act of 1965 outlaws literacy tests for voter registration and ensures oversight of the registration process by the Department of Justice.

1966
Republican Edward Brooke of Massachusetts becomes the first African American elected to the U.S. senate in eighty-five years.

Huey P. Newton and Bobby Seale found the Black Panthers in Oakland, California.

1967
In July, deadly riots erupt in Detroit, Michigan, and Newark, New Jersey.

Thurgood Marshall becomes the first African American to serve on the United States Supreme Court.

1968
On April 4, 1968, Martin Luther King, Jr., is assassinated on the balcony of the Lorraine Motel in Memphis, Tennessee. He was in Memphis to show support for striking

sanitation workers. James Earl Ray is later convicted for the murder and sentenced to serve ninety-nine years in prison.

Despite the passing of Dr. King, the Poor People's March descends on Washington in May of 1968. The march is part of the Poor People's Campaign that had been planned by King to draw attention to issues of economic inequality.

1973
Maynard Jackson of Atlanta becomes the first African American elected mayor of a major southern U.S. city.

1978
In the *Regents of the University of California v. Bakke* decision, the Supreme Court forbids the use of quota systems, but allows that race can be used as a factor in determining college admissions.

1979
In what comes to be known as "the Greensboro Massacre," five protestors are shot and killed by members of the Ku Klux Klan while organizing industrial workers there.

1983
Martin Luther King Day becomes an official federal holiday to honor the birth of the civil rights leader, who was born on January 10.

1988

Congress passes the Civil Rights Restoration Act, which requires recipients of federal funds to comply with all civil rights laws.

1989

U.S. Army General Colin Powell becomes the first African American to serve as chairman of the Joint Chiefs of Staff under President Bush.

1989

Virginia's Douglas Wilder becomes the first African American to be elected governor in the U.S.

1994

Byron De La Beckwith is convicted of the 1963 assassination of Medgar Evers.

2003

Edgar Ray Killen is convicted of three counts of manslaughter for being the ringleader of the murder of the three civil rights workers murdered in Mississippi in 1964.